♥♥♥♥♥♥♥♥♥♥♥♥♥♥♥♥♥♥♥♥♥♥

"Mollie, what happened?" Cindy insisted.

Shaking her head, her blue eyes looking as if she had just seen a ghost, Mollie handed Cindy a note written on Nicole's pink and white stationery.

"Read it." Mollie's voice was hoarse.

Puzzled, Cindy took the note.

Dear Cindy and Mollie:

Please don't let this letter upset you. I've gone to Los Angeles overnight. Tell Mom I'm with Bitsy. I promise I'll explain everything when I get back. Mom wasn't around, so I couldn't tell her.

Love, Nicole

Suddenly Cindy felt a strangeness in the pit of her stomach. She shook her head, unwilling to believe what she was thinking, and she sank down onto the bed. "Mollie, how could we have been so blind? You're right. Nicole's run off, but not because she's a spy. She's in love, and she's run off to get married."

FAWCETT GIRLS ONLY BOOKS

Sisters

THREE'S A CROWD #1

TOO LATE FOR LOVE #2

THE KISS #3

SECRETS AT SEVENTEEN #4

SISTERS

SECRETS AT SEVENTEEN

Jennifer Cole

FAWCETT GIRLS ONLY • NEW YORK

RLI: VL: Grades 5 & UP / IL: Grades 6 & UP

A Fawcett Girls Only Book
Published by Ballantine Books
Copyright © 1986 by Cloverdale Press, Inc.

Library of Congress Catalog Card Number: 86-90887

ISBN 0-449-13011-8

Manufactured in the United States of America

First Edition: July 1986

Chapter 1

"*Hey! Nicole! Wait up!*" *Bitsy chased after* her best friend, running across the football field and nearly colliding with the biggest linebacker on the Vista High football team.

"Nicole," she called again, breathless as she managed to catch up to her friend, "what's the hurry? Why didn't you stop?"

"Oh, Bitsy." Nicole flushed slightly as her blue eyes focused on Bitsy's red face. "I'm sorry. I didn't hear you."

"Didn't hear me? Nicole Lewis, practically the whole school heard me."

When Bitsy looked around, she noticed that several of the guys on the football team were watching them instead of practicing—not that

Bitsy minded, but now wasn't the time to take advantage of it. She had to talk to Nicole and find out why her friend was avoiding her these days. Still, Bitsy waved to Jeff standing on the goal line.

The team went back to work only after the coach blew the whistle and threatened extra laps.

"I said I'm sorry." Nicole continued to walk.

"Yeah, I heard." She had to use every muscle in her short legs to keep up with Nicole. "Something the matter?"

Nicole shook her head, swishing her light brown hair across her face. Bitsy was aware that, as always, Nicole looked calm and elegant in a paisley blouse and gray trousers, while Bitsy could feel the sweat on her forehead and her tights slipping down as she struggled to keep up with her friend.

"Well, then, where're you going in such a hurry? I thought we had a yearbook meeting at Pete's."

"Not today." Nicole hurried on.

"What do you mean, not today?" She grabbed Nicole's arm, forcing her to a standstill. "We have a yearbook meeting. And *you're* the editor-in-chief."

"Sorry. I can't make it today."

Stunned, Bitsy could only stare at Nicole. "What do you mean? You're the one who called the meeting!"

Nicole shrugged, realizing that Bitsy was right. "Bitsy, can you take over for me, just for today?"

"Well, I suppose so, but ..."

"Great, thanks a lot." Nicole gave Bitsy a light hug and ran for the bus, which had just pulled up to the corner.

"Nicole, wait. I want to know . . ." Bitsy started to run after her friend, but Nicole had already climbed on board.

"You're a sweetheart, Bitsy. I'll call you tonight and find out what happened," Nicole yelled through the window as the noise and exhaust fumes from the bus swallowed the rest of her words.

Bitsy could only stand there, staring at the disappearing bus and wondering what on earth was wrong with Nicole.

Mrs. Lewis was stirring the hollandaise sauce for dinner and fighting off the two cats when Mollie walked in.

"We must be having fish," she said, throwing her books on the counter, grabbing a cookie from the jar, and offering some of it to the cats, Cinders and Smokey. Cinders, who ate just about anything, quickly grabbed the sweet and proudly trotted it off to a corner, while Smokey ignored Mollie's offering as if to say "how dare you offer me human food."

"You're going to spoil those animals, Mollie."

"Not me." Mollie munched. "It's Cindy who spoils them."

"What happened to your diet? I didn't know cookies were allowed," Mom said as she opened the oven with a protective mitt. Whatever her mother was making smelled delicious. No wonder the cats were hanging around.

"Well, cookies *are* allowed." Defiantly, Mollie tossed back her long blonde hair. "It's called the junk food diet. You're allowed to eat one thing from each fast-food place once a day."

"Sounds delightful. Just don't ruin your appetite. I'm testing a new recipe." Mrs. Lewis ran a catering business, Moveable Feasts, and often tested out new recipes on her family, first.

"Well, I'm sure what we don't eat, the cats will." Mollie grabbed another cookie and headed for the hall. "Cindy or Nicole home?"

"Cindy's playing tennis with Grant, and Nicole ..." Mrs. Lewis paused, trying to think. "Nicole had some sort of meeting for the yearbook. I think they were going to the pizza place."

"Oh?" Mollie reappeared in the doorway and watched her mother for a few more minutes to make sure that she was busy. "Guess she won't be home for a couple of hours, then."

"I don't expect either of your sisters until dinner. Say, what happened to *your* meeting?"

Mollie shrugged. "Steve wasn't going, so I decided not to go."

"It's Steve this week, then. Oh, Mollie," her mother sighed, "when will you learn that you can't live your life just for boys?"

"Maybe I can and maybe I can't." Mollie reached

for the cookie jar again, but her mother pushed it out of the way. "Anyway, I've got a history paper to work on. I'm going to my room."

"All right, sweetheart."

Mollie hurried up the stairs with Winston, their Newfoundland, nipping at her heels. The large black dog began to bark as she neared Nicole's room.

"Shh, Winston." But she had prepared for this, and took out a doggie treat from her pocket. Winston adored and protected Nicole—just like everyone else, Mollie thought. It wasn't fair—especially when she and Cindy were the ones who ended up walking the dog most of the time.

Even with the treat in his mouth, the dog barked. "Sit! I'll take you out in a minute," Mollie promised.

Winston seemed to accept this and sat back and waited, his tongue hanging out as he saw the second treat in her hand.

"Okay, Winnie." Mollie threw him the extra treat. "Now, just be quiet, please. I promise I'm not doing anything wrong.'" She watched the dog chew his food. "I just want to try on Nicole's new angora sweater."

Winston gave her a quizzical look, watching her every move as she opened her sister's door.

What a difference between her room and Nicole's! Of course, being the eldest, Nicole had the biggest room, but the real difference was the decor and the neat-as-a-pin order Nicole kept it in. Mollie looked around at the Laura Ashley wallpaper and the floral spread covering the antique bed. Nicole had so much wonderful wall space, and all she had up were a few silly prints. Mollie knew they were all French paintings, although she couldn't remember the names. But Nicole, who adored everything French, could probably recite each painting's entire life history.

The bed springs creaked as Mollie sat down on the cushions and looked around in awe at the neatly organized room. It was such a contrast to her own cluttered mess. "Hello, Pepper," she said to the stuffed monkey seated on the bed.

She had closed the door so that the dog and cats couldn't get in, but she had the strange feeling that Pepper or one of the other stuffed animals Nicole had collected over the years would tell on her. That was silly—real animals didn't talk, so why should fake ones? Even so, Mollie hurried toward the drawer where Nicole kept her sweaters. That was one thing about her older sister that Mollie liked. She knew exactly where everything was in this room—although it made it more difficult to borrow things, since Mollie couldn't claim Nicole had probably just misplaced an item of clothing.

Nicole even made her bed in the morning. As far as Mollie was concerned, that was a disgusting waste of time. Why make a bed if you're going to sleep in it that night?

She opened the drawer and picked up the light blue sweater. It was the same color as her eyes, she thought as she held it against her face in the mirror. Of course, it was also the same color as Nicole's eyes.

Walking to the door, she listened for a moment to make sure that Mom was still in the kitchen. She could hear Winston's ragged breathing outside as he waited for her. Drat that dog! If Mom came into the hall and saw him there, she would know where Mollie was.

Quickly, Mollie pulled the angora sweater over her head and ruffled her long wavy blonde hair just like the models did.

The shoulders were slightly big, but that was, as Nicole was so fond of pointing out, the style in Paris. Mollie turned around, admiring herself in the mirror. The sweater was nice, but maybe it did make her look a little too top-heavy. Sighing, she wished she could trade a few of her curves for Cindy's or Nicole's height.

It was so hard to be the youngest of three girls. She wished she could snap her fingers and grow up right now. Cindy's favorite story had always been *Peter Pan,* because Cindy didn't really want to grow up, but Mollie preferred *Cinderella,* because it seemed to fit her own situation so well. After all, here she was with her two horrid elder sisters being pushed down and kept away from her prince charming. Not that her sisters were that bad, she admitted.

"Mollie! Mol? Where are you?" Mrs. Lewis's voice floated into her dreams. "You have a phone call. It's Steve Amunsen."

Steve! Calling her here at home!

Forgetting that she still wore Nicole's sweater, Mollie flung open the door of her sister's room and rushed into the hallway. Winston barked furiously, and her mother appeared at the top of the stairs.

"Mollie, isn't that your sister's?" Mrs. Lewis asked.

"Yeah, I guess." Mollie picked up the phone receiver on the hall table. "I'll talk to you about it later, okay, Mom?" she hissed, dragging the phone into her own room, where she could have some privacy.

But Mrs. Lewis continued to stand in the hall.

"Mom . . ."

"The moment you're off the phone, young lady—"

"Yes, Mom." Mollie felt the irritation rising as her stomach tightened. She hoped Steve hadn't heard her mother. She'd just die if he had.

"Hi, Steve," she said, changing her voice completely. "Do you have the algebra assignment for me?"

"Sure. Want me to read it over the phone to you, or do you want to come over and get it?"

"Oh! I'll come over," she said excitedly. "It'll only take me a few minutes on my bike. You live just off State Street, don't you?"

"Yes. How did you ..."

Mollie flushed, glad that he couldn't see her. "Oh, I ... remember when Mrs. James dropped us both off. You were let off first and I"—she shrugged—"just remembered, that's all." She wasn't going to tell him that she'd looked his address up in the phone book, or that she'd ridden her bike past his house several times last week.

"Oh. I was just on my way over to Taco Rio. Wanna meet me there instead?"

"That'd be great. See you in a few."

Mollie hung up quickly and ran to her room.

"Mollie, I want to talk to you."

"Not now, Mom. Later. I promise. I gotta meet Steve. It's important. My math assignment."

"Well, you can't wear your sister's sweater. Take it off now."

"Mom ..." Mollie frowned. "Okay, okay, I'll put it back."

She ran back to Nicole's room with Winston following close behind her and accusing her of breaking promises. "Listen, Winnie, I'm sorry. You'll just have to wait until Mom has time or until Cindy comes home."

Mollie pulled the sweater off and was about to throw it on the floor—as she usually did with her own things—but then remembered this was Nicole's room and Nicole's sweater. With an exaggerated sigh, she jerked open the drawer and began to stuff the sweater in.

The dog barked again, as if to tell her that Nicole wouldn't like that either.

"I wish all of you would stop ganging up on me. I'm only a kid," Mollie told the dog defensively. But Winston was right, she thought.

Kneeling in front of the bureau, she folded the sweater and started to place it back onto the neat pile from which she had taken it, when she saw some folded papers partially hidden in back of the drawer. Was Nicole hiding something? A secret diary?

Curious, Mollie pulled the loose sheets out. There were three of them, but they weren't diary notes at all. Just exam sheets. She looked at them, disappointed. It was odd that they were there, in the back of the drawer. Had Nicole placed them there purposely? Or had they just gotten stuck there?

If it had been her own room, Mollie would have known the answer to be the latter, but not neat Nicole. Mollie looked at the papers again and then realized why her older sister had hidden them. Nicole had nearly failed one of the tests, and the other two were low B's.

Mollie whistled under her breath and stuck the papers back inside the drawer along with the sweater.

Her sister aced almost everything. In fact, Mollie had never known Nicole to fail—ever. All of Mollie's teachers were forever comparing her with Nicole, and sometimes even with Cindy, who did pretty well, although she hardly ever studied.

As Mollie left the room, she wondered how Nicole could have failed. But she had more important things on her mind. Right now, she was determined to use her poor performance in math to her advantage—to hook Steve.

"Love–six," Cindy called as she tossed the ball over the net to Grant's side of the court. "You're not doing so well today, are you?"

Grant MacPhearson picked up the yellow ball and bounced it on the court a couple of times before answering. "It's this cold coming on. I told you before, I wasn't feeling too hot."

"Then we should have waited to play."

"I also promised you a game. Remember, loser buys at Pete's."

Cindy carelessly brushed her short sun-bleached hair off her face. "I remember, but I don't want to take unfair advantage—if you're *really* not feeling well, that is."

Grant merely grimaced and served the ball, which she deftly returned. His backhand couldn't catch it, though, and the ball landed at his feet. Frowning, he picked up the ball.

She stared at Grant and wondered what to do.

It was obvious that he was becoming more and more upset with her because she was beating him. But her one-on-one surfing competition with Grant at the beginning of the school year had taught her that she couldn't purposely lose just to soothe Grant's ego. And he had really seemed to accept defeat then with good grace. So why was he acting so childish now?

It was then that she saw Bitsy walking by—without Nicole—and dropped her racquet. "Hold on, Grant. I need to talk to Bitsy." Cindy hurried over to her sister's best friend. "Hey, where's Nicole? I thought the two of you had some sort of editorial meeting today. She was supposed to pick me up here afterward."

Bitsy just stared past her into the tennis court. Even though she was preoccupied, she couldn't help but notice Grant. The bandanna tied around his dark wavy hair emphasized his turquoise eyes, and the tennis gear, his long, muscular legs and broad shoulders. Cindy had certainly caught a hunk, Bitsy thought. Bitsy forced her thoughts back to Nicole. "Yeah, we had a meeting. Rather, I did." Bitsy frowned. "I saw her running across campus and tried to stop her, but she brushed me off and asked me to take over the meeting."

Cindy's mouth dropped open slightly. "She missed the yearbook meeting? That's not like Nicole."

"I know. She's also missed lunch with me the

last four days in a row. I've hardly seen her at all the last two weeks! None of her other friends have either." Bitsy wet her lips, as if unsure how to ask. "She hasn't said anything to you, has she? I mean, about being upset with me or something?"

Cindy shook her head.

"Hey, Cindy, what's up?" Grant crossed the court and jumped over the net as he came over to them. "Hi, Bitsy. Cindy, aren't we playing?"

She looked at Grant, standing impatiently, hand on hip, and then at Bitsy. "I think something's wrong. I'd better go home." This was as good an excuse as any to end this silly game.

"If you leave now, you'll forfeit the game. I win, then."

"Yeah, I know. Don't worry, it's okay."

Cindy quickly put on her gray sweats and grabbed her tennis racquet. "Look, I'll see you at lunch tomorrow. Okay?"

Grant nodded. "Are we still going to Pete's after school tomorrow?"

"Sure."

Cindy let herself out of the court and started toward the bike racks. Bitsy followed closely behind her.

"Is there really something wrong? I mean, is that why Nicole's acting so strange?"

Cindy shook her head. "No, I doubt anything's wrong, Bitsy, but I'll find out."

Chapter 2

*T*he beach was deserted as Cindy rode by on her way home. She couldn't help wonder what was happening between Bitsy and Nicole. Come to think of it, her sister had been a little preoccupied lately, and Cindy had dismissed it as problems at school—but now that she thought of it, she realized Nicole never had problems at school. Even when she broke up with her boyfriend Mark recently, it had hardly seemed to affect her. Nicole never had any problems at all—or, at least, none that Cindy could remember. And everything about Nicole was perfect. Recalling the way Nicole had "parented" Cindy and Mollie during their parents' trip to Japan, Cindy knew just how imperfect Nicole could be. Sometimes she was so darn bossy. But usually, Cindy admitted, she was a fairly nice older sister.

Still, it upset her the way Mom sometimes compared her with Nicole, trying to get her to read more books like Nicole, or to dress like Nicole, or be more responsible like Nicole. But Cindy wasn't like Nicole, or like Mollie for that matter, and she really didn't want to be like either of her sisters. Why should she?

Stopping her bike near the beach shack, Cindy watched the waves roll in. She wished she had her surfboard with her. Nicole probably wasn't even home yet. She hadn't been around very much lately. If she hadn't been with Bitsy or any of her other friends, where had she been going?

Cindy began to pedal back toward the house and turned her thoughts to Grant. She really liked him—they enjoyed doing the same things—but there were times lately when he seemed so ... well, so much like a boy. Not that boys were bad, but once they became your boyfriend, things changed. And all of a sudden everyone was prying into your life, trying to find out how you were getting along.

That was something Cindy failed to understand. She didn't think it was so important to have a boyfriend, yet that was all her friends seemed to think about anymore. That and getting a date for whatever dance was coming up. Like right now, there was some big dance being held off-campus, and all anyone talked about was who was going with whom, or who hadn't been invited yet. Already her friends were bugging her about whether or not she was going with Grant.

Then she thought of the way she felt when Grant had his arm around her, when he smiled at her. Well, maybe it wasn't so bad having Grant as a boyfriend. She certainly didn't feel that way about Duffy or any of her other friends who were boys. With them, she just felt comfortable, not special.

She shrugged and pedaled harder. If nothing else, she had to talk to Nicole and get her opinion about Grant. Since Nicole had broken up with Mark, she had dated lots of different guys. Maybe Nicole could explain to her why things get so complicated when boys become boyfriends.

Cindy parked her bike in the garage and went into the house.

Slamming the door behind her, Cindy immediately went to the kitchen. No one was there but Cinders, who jumped up on the table for Cindy to pick her up, purring her welcome greeting and rubbing against Cindy's arm.

"Hello, baby," Cindy picked up the cat and hugged her, receiving in return a wet, rough tongue kiss. "You smell of fish." Cindy picked up the cover of the rattling pot and turned the heat down for her mother. Still holding the cat, she opened the refrigerator door and peered inside.

Even though it was nearly dinnertime, Cindy began to take out a piece of quiche but quickly put it back and closed the door when she heard her mother's footsteps.

"Mom, is Nicole or Mollie home?"

Mrs. Lewis came into the kitchen, followed by Winston, who was determined not to be left out of the fun. With a bark and a huge wet tongue, he leaped on Cindy, nearly knocking her over.

"I think he wants to go out. Can you take him, honey? Mollie was home earlier and she was supposed to walk him, but she disappeared. Something about a math assignment and another boy, I think."

Cindy made a face. "Mom, Mollie's a real pest with some of the guys. Can't you talk to her? It's embarrassing."

Mrs. Lewis smiled and shrugged. "Talking to her about not thinking so much about boys is as good as talking to you about thinking about them a bit more."

"Oh, Mom, it's not the same." Cindy picked up Winston's leash. She wasn't in the mood to talk about boys. "What's so great about a dance, anyway?" she muttered.

The dog jumped up, knowing she meant to take him out.

"Come on, boy. You and I will go to the dance together." Cindy left the house before her mother could ask what she meant.

*   *   *

Mollie braked her bike outside of Taco Rio, snapped her lock closed, and quickly glanced through the windows to check if Steve was there yet. But he wasn't. That was strange. He had promised to meet her here, and he lived a lot closer than she did. Well, she thought, combing her hair in the reflection from the window, he'd be here soon.

Approaching the counter, Mollie realized that she had forgotten to bring her allowance with her. Well, maybe Steve would be sweet and buy her a burrito. Her stomach growled. Then Mollie realized she'd be having dinner soon, and Mom wouldn't like her to eat before dinner—even if she was hungry and even if a boy was treating her. Oh, well, she'd settle for a Coke.

Glancing around, Mollie immediately noticed all the older guys from the junior and senior class there. Brushing her blonde bangs off her forehead, she smiled at one of the junior boys, who was looking her way. He tapped the seat beside him and Mollie smiled again. She probably would have gone over to sit with him if she hadn't seen Steve walking up the street just then.

"You getting something to eat?" Steve asked as he joined her at the counter.

Mollie shook her head. "We're having supper soon. But I wouldn't mind a Coke."

"Yeah, me too. It's hot out there."

Waiting in line, Mollie glanced nervously at the mirror to check her appearance. She wished she had taken the time to put on a little more makeup. She noticed, with satisfaction, that Steve had a nice profile.

"Do you want the whole week's assignment or just yesterday's?" Steve turned to ask, catching Mollie looking at herself in the mirror.

Mollie blushed and turned to Steve. "Oh, I . . . Yesterday's is all I need."

Steve handed over a sheet with the assignment written on it. Mollie stared at it blankly. "But I wonder." She lowered her lashes. "Could you explain it to me? I mean, I'm having a lot of problems with math."

"Uh, sure." Steve cleared his throat and pushed his glasses up onto his nose as the Cokes were placed in front of him. "But not now. I have to get home." He put out the money for his soda and grabbed the cup. "Catch me during study hall tomorrow, and if you don't still understand it, we can go over it."

Mollie could only stare after him as he disappeared. Why had he come all the way to Taco Rio just to take away a Coke? And he hadn't even paid for hers.

When Cindy returned home with the dog, her mom was still in the kitchen preparing supper.

"Mollie and Nicole not back yet?"

"No, they're not. Would you please set the table for dinner?"

"Mom, that's not fair. It's Nicole's night for setting the table. I walked Winston. I have homework to do."

"Well, Nicole's not here, and somebody has to set the table, so you're elected, Cindy. This is a family—that means we all pitch in."

"Yeah, Mom. But the family includes Nicole. Where is she, anyway?"

Mrs. Lewis sighed. "I don't know. I can't keep up with all of you these days." She stirred the soup. "I think she had a yearbook meeting this afternoon."

"Oh," Cindy said, picking up Smokey and hugging the purring cat.

"Use the blue dishes, Cindy."

Cindy made a face and went to the cabinet.

"Come on, guys." Cindy let the cats into the dining room.

Obediently, the cats followed.

The door slammed as Mollie came into the house.

"I don't understand it. I just don't understand it. He didn't even buy me a drink."

"Who didn't? That boy?" Mrs. Lewis came in and gave her daughter a hug. "It will be all right, Mollie. One of these days you'll find someone who will be just right for you."

"Yeah." Mollie sat down, her chin in her hands. "But when?"

Cindy made a face. "Who cares? Just help me set the table."

"It's Nicole's turn," Mollie protested.

"Tell me about it." Cindy handed her the cups. "You know, Nicole gets away with murder lately. She's never here. She's *supposedly* at a yearbook meeting. At least that's what she told Mom."

"What do you mean? She lied to Mom?" Mollie hissed.

Cindy shrugged and folded the napkins. "Bitsy told me today that Nicole left her in the lurch and didn't come to the meeting. She called. Bitsy had to chair the meeting, and Nicole wouldn't tell her why."

"That's not like Nicole, but then neither is ..." She paused with a fork midair and a strange look on her face. "I wonder what's up?"

"What are you talking about? What do you know that I don't?"

Mollie peeked out of the dining room to make sure their mother wasn't around. "I was in Nicole's room earlier, and—"

Winston romped into the room, almost as if he knew what Mollie was about to say. Mollie made a face at the dog.

"I found some of her tests hidden in her sweater drawer."

Cindy stared at her sister. "Tests? Why would Nicole hide her tests?"

"Because she almost failed them!"

The cup dropped from Cindy's hand. She was glad it didn't break. She'd hate to have to explain it to Mom. "I don't believe it. Nicole failed a test?"

"Well, almost, and not one, three. Who knows how many other tests she's failed? Something's going on."

Cindy shook her head. "I don't understand. Anyway, why would she hide them? Mom and Dad would probably understand."

Mollie shrugged. She was about to respond as she heard the front door open.

"Anyone home? Is dinner ready?" Nicole asked both questions within the space of a few seconds. *"Bon soir."* She floated into the dining room, smiling. Obviously, she had totally forgotten that it was her night to set the table. Cindy could only glare at her sister.

Hearing her oldest daughter, Mrs. Lewis came into the room.

"Dinner ready, Mom? I have plans for the evening."

"Nicole, I thought we were going to work on your college applications. Where are you going?"

Nicole shifted her books from one arm to the other, avoiding her sisters' stares. "I have to meet with the yearbook people again."

"But you just did that this afternoon."

"*C'est vrai.* I know." Nicole shrugged. "But we didn't get everything done." She hurried from the room as Cindy and Mollie looked at each other in amazement.

"You're right. There is definitely something strange going on. And I'm going to find out what it is." Cindy put the remaining plates on the table and determinedly followed her older sister up the stairs.

Cindy knocked at Nicole's door, which was closed. "Can I come in?" she asked, opening the door before Nicole had time to refuse.

"If you want." Nicole sat on the bed, writing in a notebook.

"I, uh, met Bitsy on the way home from the tennis courts," Cindy said as she looked around the room, trying to see if there was anything out of the ordinary.

"That's nice."

"She was upset."

Nicole continued to write. She didn't even look up.

"I thought you guys were best friends."

"We are."

"It doesn't matter to you that Bitsy was upset and you're the cause?"

Nicole glanced up quickly and then returned to her writing. "I'm the cause? How? Bitsy's always upset about something. She's like Mollie—imagining dragons around every corner."

Cindy sighed. Her sister was not going to make things any easier. "Bitsy said you hadn't met her for your usual lunch and study breaks in nearly a week. And that you hardly ever talked to her. She's beginning to think something's wrong."

"Nothing's wrong," Nicole snapped. "Really, Cindy. I just have to finish this." She pointed to her book. "I'm very busy and I can't take the time to talk about Bitsy's imaginary problems." She stood as if to escort her sister from the room.

"But what should I tell Bitsy when I see her? She's going to want to know if I talked to you."

"You can tell her we're still friends and that she's being silly. I'm just busy. There's nothing wrong!" Nicole's face reddened slightly with her insistence. "Will you just leave me alone? I've got to finish this before tonight."

"What is it?" Cindy tried to peer over Nicole's shoulder, but her older sister slammed the book shut.

"I'll tell you when I'm good and ready to tell you. Now, weren't you setting the table?"

"Yeah, I was. And you owe me one. It's your night and you weren't home to do it. Mom asked me."

"Okay, okay, so I owe you one. I'll do it for you next week. I promise. Now, if you don't mind, Cindy—"

But before either of the girls could move, the shrill sound of the ringing phone cut the air.

Grabbing the notebook from the bed, Nicole jumped up. "I'll get it!" she cried as she flew past her sister and out into the hallway. "Don't anyone touch that. It's for me."

Mollie, entering the room in the wake of Nicole's hasty exit, shook her head. To Cindy she said, "Well, did you ask her? What did she say?"

Cindy shrugged. Nicole hadn't said anything strange, but she certainly had acted strange, as if she were hiding something. "Something is definitely going on, and I don't like it."

Chapter 3

"*Maybe Nicole's in some kind of trouble,*" Mollie said. "Maybe someone's blackmailing her or something. She was writing something in a notebook just before the phone rang, wasn't she?" Mollie's face lit up with glee as Cindy scowled at her. "Maybe it was some sort of secret plan. Maybe she's spying. She does have that strange friend at the naval base. Maybe he's her secret contact."

"Oh, Mollie. Be serious. You and your imagination. I doubt she's in any trouble, but I do think we need to investigate and get her to tell us what's up before Mom and Dad find out, or she flunks out of school. Come on." Cindy dragged her younger sister out of the room. "We can't stay in here."

"But we might find something useful. Something that will tell us ..."

"First, let's try talking to Nicole once more. Maybe if she realizes we know something, she'll admit whatever she's doing or why she's lying."

"Not if she's spying for the Russians, she won't," Mollie giggled.

"Oh, Mollie, shut up."

Cindy shut the door firmly behind her and hurried halfway down the steps, then stopped. Nicole was on the phone in the hallway, but she was talking so softly that it was impossible to hear what she was saying.

"What are you girls doing?" Mrs. Lewis appeared at the bottom of the stairs as Nicole swirled around to see her two sisters standing below her on the steps.

Mollie twisted her little finger around a lock of her blonde hair as she looked down at her mother. "Nothing. Just waiting for Nicole to get off the phone so we can have dinner." She smiled at Nicole.

"Can't anyone have any privacy around here?" Nicole slammed down the phone. "That happened to be a very important call." She glared at her younger sisters. "Mother, you really need to teach these two some manners."

Flying down the stairs past her sisters, Nicole grabbed a roll off the dining room table.

"Hey, Mom, she's—" Mollie began.

"Nicole, wait for dinner. Your father will be home in five minutes and then we can eat."

Nicole kissed her mother's cheek. "Sorry, I can't wait. I'll grab something to eat later. I've got an important meeting now."

"But Nicole," Mrs. Lewis protested.

"It's an emergency meeting. The yearbook is having trouble, Mom."

Nicole was out the door, closing it behind her before her mother could say anything more.

"Mom would never have let us do that," Mollie whispered to Cindy. "It's not fair."

Cindy pressed her lips together in a thin line. Mollie was right, but that wasn't the problem now. She bent down and petted Cinders, who was purring at her feet. "I'd still like to know what's going on."

Mollie looked to make sure their mother wasn't in sight and grabbed one of the buttermilk rolls. "I told you. She's been hired as a Russian spy."

It was after eleven when Nicole finally came home.

"Late meeting, dear?" Mrs. Lewis asked.

"Yes. I'm exhausted."

"No homework, Nicole?" Mr. Lewis looked up from the blueprints he was studying.

"Did it during study hall, Dad." She kissed both her parents. "See you in the morning."

Her mother nodded and Nicole hurried up the steps before they could ask her any more questions.

It was a relief to reach the safety of her room and to shut out her family.

"Hello, Pepper." Nicole picked up the threadbare stuffed monkey. "How are you?" She hugged the animal, pretending it had answered. She knew she was too old for dolls, but her animals were her link with the past. Mom was forever trying to get them put up in the attic, but Nicole couldn't bear the idea of their getting torn and dusty. Besides, she wanted them in good condition to pass on to her children when she married.

Sitting at her dressing table, brushing her hair out, Nicole studied her features in the mirror. When she was married, she planned to have lots of children and vowed to respect their privacy. She was almost eighteen years old and she had a right to have a few secrets from her family and her friends. They needed to learn some respect.

She picked up Pepper again. "I will never leave you, *ma cherie,*" she told the monkey. "Even without your one eye, I adore you. *Je t'a—*"

"Who is it?" Nicole put the monkey on the table as she heard the knock at her door.

"Me," Mollie called out. "Can I come in?"

"Door's open."

Mollie appeared in the doorway, wearing her pink ruffled nightshirt. Her blue eyes looked even bigger with her long wavy hair pulled back from her face. Sometimes it alarmed Nicole to see how quickly her little sister was growing up.

"What's wrong? I thought you'd be in bed ages ago."

"I was." Mollie shrugged. "But I was reading *Seventeen* and it made me think."

"About?"

"About things." Mollie sat down with her legs folded under her on her sister's floral-print bedspread as Nicole spun around.

"Like?"

"Steve, for example. He asked me to meet him at Taco Rio to give me my math assignment—and then he didn't even buy me a Coke. I must have done something wrong, because the magazine says— "

"Mollie, you can't believe everything a magazine says. And you can't expect every boy to fall in love with you."

"But they fall in love with you. I want to grow up. I'm tired of being treated like a kid. Arlene already has a boyfriend. Why can't I?"

Nicole snorted. "Some boyfriend. Mollie . . ."

She turned to see Mollie hugging her knees to her chest, like a child. "Mollie, don't worry. Things will be right when they're right. After all, you're my sister. How can you be anything but successful?" Nicole teased.

Mollie shrugged. "Cindy's your sister, too. And she's not doing so well with Grant these days. I mean, they're perfect for each other and she's being an idiot. Maybe I'm being an idiot, too."

"Mollie, you may be an idiot, but I'm sure you didn't do anything wrong with Steve. Maybe he was in a hurry. I mean, he didn't say he was going to buy you something. You can't figure that every guy you meet is going to treat you. Some men are ... well ... some aren't as mature as others."

"Was Mark mature?"

Nicole shook her head. "I don't think any boy in high school is really mature. Girls mature faster than boys. Maybe Steve's just too young."

"You think I ought to go after Paul Whitman, then?"

"Paul Whitman?" It was Nicole's turn to be surprised. "Mollie, Paul Whitman's a senior. He's the star of the football team."

"I know. But he's older than me, and he's certainly mature."

Nicole shook her head and made a face. "He's older than you, but just because a guy is a senior doesn't mean he's mature." She leaned over and tousled her sister's hair. "Just don't worry. The right man will come for you when you're ready. Now, it's time for both of us to go to bed."

But Mollie hadn't learned anything yet. She decided to try another tactic. "Nicole, what really happened with you and Mark?"

Nicole shrugged. "Mollie, I really don't want to talk about him."

"But I was sure you were going to marry him. Wouldn't it have been nice to get married right after high school?"

"I don't know." Nicole sat down beside Mollie. "Sure, sometimes I think it would be nice. Then you wouldn't have to worry about your future. But then there's a lot of other things to do, like college and travel."

"Where do you want to go, besides France?"

"Oh, Spain, Italy, Austria, Switzerland ..." Nicole's voice trailed off.

"Ever think of going to Russia?"

"Russia?" Nicole's brow creased. "I never thought of that. Sure. I guess it would be interesting. It's certainly different."

"But—" Mollie interrupted.

"The point is that there are lots of places and lots of boys, too."

"I guess." Mollie unfolded her legs and stood, but paused at the door. "How come you're keeping your door locked? You didn't used to."

Nicole shrugged. "It wasn't locked just now."

"Yeah, because you thought I was asleep."

Nicole didn't answer. "There's no reason I can't lock my door occasionally, if I want to. I mean, it really doesn't matter if my door is locked or not. Anyway, I don't want you in here borrowing my things without my knowing about it."

"Oh, I didn't mean that." Mollie was all wide-eyed innocence, hoping that her mother (or Pepper) hadn't told on her. "I was only curious." She took a quick look around the room, but nothing looked different from before. She gave it one last try. "Can I read your poetry sometime? I mean all that gooey stuff you wrote to Mark."

"Why?" Nicole was suspicious. "You didn't like it before, when I was dating him."

Mollie shrugged. "I want to write some poetry to Steve, like you did. Maybe—"

"Mollie, you'll have to write your own poetry."

"Do you still write poetry? I mean, this afternoon, Cindy saw you writing in your notebook. I thought . . ."

"I was making some notes for the yearbook meeting. That's all." Nicole began to close the door against her sister's questions. "Good night, Mol. See you in the morning." Winston tried to slip into the room as Mollie was leaving.

"Go away, boy," Nicole edged him out along with her sister. The door closed firmly behind them, leaving Mollie and Winston standing out in the hall.

The dog looked up at Mollie in wonderment.

"Yeah, I know, Winston. She's in a bad mood."

The next morning, Cindy was still eating breakfast when Mollie came down. Mollie stared in amazement at Cindy's breakfast: cereal, eggs, toast, orange juice, even bacon! Glumly slicing a grapefruit, Mollie joined her sister at the table.

"Nicole gone?"

"Somewhere." Cindy poured herself another glass of juice, and buttered her toast. "Mom wants you to take the roast out before you leave."

"Yeah, okay." She drank from her sister's glass. "I talked to Nicole last night. She tell you?"

Cindy shook her head.

"I'll bet you ten dollars that I'm right," Mollie said with an air of importance as she broke off a piece of Cindy's bacon.

"About?"

"Russia. The spy business."

Cindy rolled her eyes and pushed her plate in front of Mollie. "What exactly did she say?"

Mollie gave her a mysterious smile. "That she'd like to travel. And that she'd like to visit Russia."

"What else did she say?" Cindy was suspicious. "Are you sure you didn't put the words in her mouth?"

Mollie shook her head. "Of course not. I was just asking her about boys and—"

"Is that all you ever think of?" Cindy poured a bowl of milk for the cats.

Mollie shrugged. "Sometimes I think about schoolwork. But not often." Changing the subject, she asked, "Are you going with Grant to the Alta California Ball?"

Cindy stared at her sister. Why was everyone so interested in her social life? "What?"

"Oh, Cin, don't tell me you don't know about it.

It's the party of the semester. The frat that Grant's in gives this huge party in the Mission Gardens every year and people dress up in old Spanish costumes. It's really neat."

"How would you know?"

"'Cuz, I heard," Mollie sighed. "Steve's in the same fraternity. I wish he'd ask me. I'd love to go. I've got the perfect outfit to wear. Nicole's Spanish shawl, and a comb and mantilla from the mission store. All I need is a dress."

"I've already heard all about it. Why don't you just concentrate on your schoolwork for a change?" Cindy finished her milk, lifted her backpack, and started toward the door. "Tell you what. If Grant asks me, I'll let you go with him instead."

Mollie's mouth dropped open. "Are you serious?"

"Sure, right now I am." Cindy smiled at her sister. "But then again I might change my mind this afternoon. I have to treat him to a pizza because I lost at tennis yesterday."

"You actually let him win?"

Cindy glared at her sister. "I've changed my mind already. No, Mollie, I didn't *let* him win. I had to leave because Bitsy came by and she was worried about Nicole. I left the game." She pulled out her Walkman and lifted the earphones to her head. "I've more important things on my mind than silly chatter. I promised I'd meet Bitsy at the cafeteria this morning and tell her what I found out. Though I haven't the faintest idea what I'm going to say."

"Well, don't let on that we think Nicole might be a spy."

Cindy sighed. When would her little sister grow up and stop these fantasies? Then she realized that if Nicole really was in trouble—not spying, of course, but some other kind of trouble—Mollie might be right about being careful with Bitsy. "Yeah, I'll be careful what I say." The door slammed after her.

After finishing Cindy's breakfast, Mollie put the dishes in the sink and took out the roast.

The silence of the house unnerved her. She thought again about Nicole and how strange her older sister had acted. Something was definitely troubling Nicole, and it wasn't just a few failed exams.

Telling herself that she was only heading up the steps to get the books from her room, Mollie stopped outside Nicole's door. She was sure if she could read that notebook Nicole had been frantically writing in, her questions would be answered.

Mollie's hand went to the door. She looked down the hall at Winston watching her.

"Don't look at me like that! I'm not going to borrow anything. I'm not doing anything wrong."

Winston contined looking at her as if to blame her for everything that went wrong.

Nevertheless, Mollie decided to brave the show-down. After all, Winston's bark was worse than his bite. Anyway, even if he tried to tattle on her, no one was home to believe him.

"Blast!" she cursed. Winston or not, there was no way she could get into the room. Nicole had locked the door.

Grabbing her books from her room, Mollie vowed that before the end of the week she'd have the answer to Nicole's secret.

Chapter 4

At Pete's, Grant and Cindy shared a double cheese pizza with anchovies.

"At least you're a good sport, Cindy." He leaned over and placed his tanned hand over hers. "You know how to lose gracefully. Most of the time," he teased.

Cindy eyed him as she tucked a long string of cheese into her mouth and deliberately chewed. She wasn't going to get into an argument with him now, though as she looked at the pizza, she could easily imagine it dripping down all over his handsome face.

"You're smiling. That's good. You haven't smiled much lately. I thought maybe you'd lost your sense of humor."

Cindy, impatiently tapping her foot under the table, was having a hard time keeping her temper. Why was Grant making such a big deal out of a silly tennis game?

"Listen, Cindy, I wanted to ask you—" Grant began.

But Cindy spied Duffy's lanky figure, red hair, and freckles. As he approached their table, Cindy removed her hand from Grant's. He probably wanted to mooch some of the pizza, which was just as well for Grant, because if she continued this conversation, she was going to strangle him.

"Hi, guys." Duffy came over and slapped both Cindy and Grant on the back before he picked up a piece of pizza. "What's new?"

Cindy laughed good-naturedly as her friend sat down beside Grant. "Gotta go." She stood before Grant could stop her. "See you both at swim practice."

"What happened there?" Duffy asked Grant.

Grant shook his head. "I don't know. I was about to ask her to the Alta California Ball when suddenly she got all strange on me." He picked up the last piece of the pizza before Duffy ate it all.

Try as they might to question her, or trip her up, neither Mollie nor Cindy managed to get any information from their older sister. Nicole was definitely being silent and mysterious.

Early Saturday morning when Cindy came down for breakfast, she found Nicole already up, drinking coffee and pacing the kitchen.

"Something the matter, Nicole?"

"What?"

Cindy shrugged as she took out the milk and orange juice. "I know when you're upset. Sure you don't want to talk about it?"

Nicole paused for a moment and sipped some of her coffee. Her lips parted as if she planned to say something but changed her mind.

"Mom know you're drinking her Colombian coffee?"

"Of course. She made the pot of coffee before she went out this morning. I doubt that she would've prepared a whole pot just for herself. She knows I prefer the Parisian espresso, but ..."

Cindy thumbed her nose at her sister. Sometimes Nicole, with her Frenchified ways, really got to her. It was obvious, however, that something was the matter. Nicole never got up this early on a weekend. And Nicole wasn't usually this cranky for no reason.

"You going somewhere this morning?"

"No." Nicole's voice cut the air like a knife.

"Sorry I asked." Cindy backed off, and then decided to try again. "Well, you don't usually wear makeup on Saturday mornings. And you don't usually get up so early. Some new guy you want to impress?"

Nicole pressed her lips together and shook her head. Cindy could tell that she had just washed her hair, because the scent of the lilac soap Nicole always used pervaded the air.

"I told you, I'm not doing anything special."

"Then what are you waiting for?"

"Nothing."

"Why are you pacing?"

Nicole shrugged and poured nearly half the carton of milk into her coffee.

Seeing that her sister wasn't going to answer, Cindy sipped her own milk and then carefully asked, "Nicole, what ... I mean, do you ever see Mark?"

"Mark?" Nicole looked surprised. "No. Why?"

"Well, I was wondering ... I mean, you and he were pretty close. What happened? You never really told me."

Nicole shrugged. "I didn't think you were interested. Nothing happened." She smiled at her sister's puzzled look. "I mean, I liked him and all, but didn't ... we didn't ..." She waved her hand, gesturing, and her face took on a dreamy expression. "He was nice, but when you fall in love there are"—she sighed—"special sparks that come between you and him." Nicole smiled at her sister again. "You'll understand when you're older, Cindy. Why's everybody asking about Mark all of a sudden?" She finished her coffee.

"What are your plans for the day?"

"Going to the beach." Cindy poured some milk into her cereal bowl. "Looks like a real hot day—the surf, I mean," she said, noticing her sister's quizzical expression. She paused and watched her sister. "Bitsy's joining Anna, Carey, and me. Now that you haven't been spending any time with her, I guess she feels left out."

"Bitsy?" Nicole's blue eyes went big. "Why? I mean, she has other friends besides me. And she's not even in your crowd. You never really liked her before."

Cindy shrugged. "She wants me to teach her how to surf, and I guess she also wants to know what's going on with you. You have been acting rather strange lately. You've canceled tons of things with her. The two of you used to do everything together." Cindy paused. "What should I tell her?"

"Tell her . . ." Nicole paused. "Tell her that I've more important things to do." Her eyes shone as she touched her younger sister's arm lightly. "Oh, Cindy. I have great plans. And I want them to be a surprise."

"What plans?"

Nicole sighed. "I can't tell you yet. But I will. I promise. Soon."

"But why can't you tell me now?" Cindy stared at her older sister. "What have you done?"

Nicole shook her head. "I told you. I'll explain it all. Very soon. And tell Bitsy that she should understand. Why is everyone so nosy all of a sudden?"

Cindy left the table and followed Nicole into the hall. "But what should she understand? If you're having a problem ..."

"Really, don't worry."

Before Cindy could say anything more, the phone shrilled and Nicole broke away, running to get it.

Cindy stared after her sister. It was no use trying to listen to the conversation, because Nicole was speaking French—and Cindy was barely passing Spanish. She turned around and cursed Cinders as the cat jumped down from the table and knocked over Cindy's milk.

"You stupid animal." Cindy grabbed a handful of paper towels to mop up the milk. She grabbed her knapsack, loaded it with food from the refrigerator, and buckled it shut.

"Where are you going?" Cindy asked Nicole again as the older girl ran through the kitchen pausing only long enough to put her coffee cup in the sink.

"Out. Tell Mom I'll be back by dinner."

"But Nicole ..." Cindy could only stand there, watching through the window as Nicole hopped into the car and drove off.

Soon they were going to find out what was happening with her—very soon. Meanwhile, Cindy sniffed the coffee in the pot and decided she wasn't ready to be grown up yet if it meant drinking that stuff. She picked up the morning paper and turned to the sports section as she finished her cereal.

It was barely a half hour later when the phone rang again. Cindy was on her way out to meet her friends at the beach. Maybe it would be for Nicole, and she could find out what her sister was doing.

No such luck. The call was for Nicole, but then eighty percent of the calls coming to the Lewis household were for Nicole. It was Gabriella (Cindy suspected the girl's real name was Gertrude or something else equally as stupid) from the French Club, inquiring about Nicole's health.

"What do you mean she hasn't been to French Club meetings for two weeks now? She's president."

Cindy listened to the girl at the other end tell her about the excuses Nicole had made. Cindy knew that her sister had never had to come home early because of a sick dog or because she helped her mother. Cindy was always the one who took care of Winston's problems, and her mother had all the hired help she needed for her catering business.

"Listen, Gabriella, I'll tell Nicole that you called and that you were concerned about her. I'm sure she'll be back to normal by next week."

"Oh. That will be lovely. *Au revoir*." The girl's phony French accent was even worse than Nicole's.

"Yeah, *au revoir*," Cindy repeated. She turned to see Mollie, still in her pink ruffled nightgown, watching her. "About time you got up."

"Why? You don't have to wait for me."

"No, but I want to talk to you—about Nicole."

When Cindy left for the beach, Mollie said she'd probably join her as soon as she woke up. It was just one of those days, Mollie thought, when she didn't want to wake up. It had been nearly four days since Steve had given her the math assignment, and she'd seen him in class and sometimes in the hall, but he hadn't said a word to her. With the big party coming up shortly, she had to work fast if she wanted him to take her.

She sighed and wondered if Paul Whitman was in the frat holding the dance. She'd have to ask Nicole.

Pouring her juice, Mollie thought about who Nicole would go with, since Mark was no longer in the picture. She knew her older sister would be going with someone. After all, Mollie thought— somewhat proudly—Nicole was one of the most popular girls at school. With a sigh, Mollie wished some of Nicole's charm and ease with boys would rub off on her. Cindy, on the other hand, was okay as far as a sister went, but she doubted that Cindy even thought about a dance the way a girl was supposed to think about a dance. Cindy would probably think about it in terms of great exercise.

If only she had some magical formula to get Steve to ask her, or at least find out what his plan was. It was so difficult trying to decide how to act. Was Steve just playing a game and waiting to see how long she could hold out, or what? *Teen Miss* said that boys sometimes did just that because they were shy. Even though Steve didn't seem the shy type, one never knew.

She heard the clunk of the mail as it dropped through the slot. Maybe her new issue of *Seventeen* would be here. Maybe it would tell her how to handle Steve. She hurried to the hall.

There were no magazines, but there was a letter from Marcella, the French girl who had attended Vista last year as an exchange student. She and Nicole had been good friends and wrote often, but as Mollie held the letter up to the light, she wondered if this could have anything to do with Nicole's strange behavior.

Shaking the envelope produced no results.

She didn't dare steam it open.

Staring at the letter, Mollie decided that Marcella couldn't be involved in whatever it was that Nicole was involved in, since the girl wasn't even in Santa Barbara now and couldn't be making those weird phone calls or causing her sister to miss all of her club meetings.

Mail in hand, Mollie started up the stairs. Winston bounded up behind her and then ran ahead of her, pausing at the door to Nicole's room.

"No, I'm not going in there, Winston."

The dog whimpered slightly and then, lifting a huge paw, he pushed against the door, which opened. Mollie's mouth dropped for a moment as Nicole's letter fluttered to the ground. She paused to pick it up. Why was the door open? Why wasn't it locked?

For the past few days, Nicole had kept the door locked, and according to Cindy's report this morning, today should have been no different. Mollie wondered—but only for a moment. She wasn't going to pass up a chance to look into Nicole's room. Who knew when her sister would forget to lock the door again?

"Thanks, Winston." She slipped inside the room.

There was no question about it. Something was definitely upsetting Nicole. The bed hadn't even been made. Mollie could understand that, if it were her own room, or even Cindy's. But Nicole? No, it didn't make any sense at all.

As she started to open the bottom drawer where she had first discovered the incriminating tests, she heard footsteps on the stairs ... and they were headed her way.

Mollie prayed that it was only her mother or Cindy, but she couldn't take any chances. Besides, if Mom found her in Nicole's room, she'd be mad at her as well. Mollie couldn't risk that. She didn't want to tell Mom that Nicole was in trouble until she had some proof.

Quickly, Mollie ducked into the closet. She was still clutching the letter from Marcella.

No sooner had Mollie sat down among the shoes, kneeling so that she could see through the peep-hole, than she heard the door to the room open.

"Now where did I put those photos?" Nicole said out loud.

Mollie held her breath and remained silent as she watched her older sister pacing back and forth, picking up papers, looking in drawers.

For an awful moment, as Mollie prayed hard, it seemed that Nicole might come into the closet.

Mollie's prayers were answered when the phone in the hall rang. Nicole went out to answer it and returned to the room, dragging the phone with her.

Pressing her ear to the keyhole, Mollie tried to hear what was being said. Clenching her fist, she cursed. She wasn't close enough! All she could make out was a name—Alain.

Mollie pressed her lips together. That didn't sound like a Russian name, but one never knew.

"Oui, oui," Nicole said into the phone. "I'm on my way now. I have the photos. I'll be over soon."

Photos! Mollie gasped, nearly giving herself away. Pictures! She was right. Nicole *was* being black-mailed. No, that wasn't right; in that case "they" would have the photos, not Nicole!

She remained hidden, watching as Nicole wrote something on the pad of paper and then tore the top sheet off. She saw Nicole shuffle through an envelope and smile.

"Winston? Winston?" Nicole called to the dog. "You want to go for a ride?"

The dog bounded into the room, barking excitedly, and ran toward the closet.

"If you pull open this door, Winston," Mollie said under her breath, "so help me, I'll never take you for a walk again."

"Come on, Winston. Let's go." Nicole left the room.

Mollie waited a few minutes and then left the closet. She had to find out where Nicole was going and follow her. But how? If Nicole was driving, she could be headed anywhere—even into Los Angeles!

Mollie went over to the table and took the pad that Nicole had written on.

With a pencil, she lightly began to rub over the sheet left on the pad. The address appeared. It was a trick she had learned from watching the detective shows. The address wasn't familiar. She'd have to find out where it was and go there on her own.

Paper in hand, Mollie hurried to her room to dress and then, recalling she still had the letter from Marcella, went back and placed it under Nicole's closed door.

Chapter 5

*W*hen she checked the street map, Mollie was relieved to find that her sister wasn't going to Los Angeles. The address Nicole had written down was located in the elegant section of Montecito, one of Santa Barbara's suburbs. She knew the area because Liam Kensington, one of the cutest lifeguards at the beach, lived there.

Mollie found her heart pounding quickly as she wondered if she'd run into him today. But even as she pulled on her hot-pink sweatshirt, Mollie frowned. She was riding her bike into Montecito to see if she could find out what Nicole was doing, not to meet Liam. Still, she couldn't help putting on some eye shadow, liner, and mascara.

Wrapping a bandanna around her head, Mollie

adjusted her blonde hair into a pony tail. She realized that she'd better hurry if she wanted to catch up with Nicole, but she couldn't resist checking herself in the mirror one more time. There was no sense taking chances—she might run into Liam after all.

Hurrying outside, she quickly rolled her bike out of the garage.

For a few moments she sat outside the house, balancing on the bike while she studied the map. Probably the best way would be to ride directly up State Street, past the shopping mall and the library, and behind the Mission. From there she'd take one of the country roads, since she certainly couldn't ride her bike on the freeway.

By the time Mollie reached the proper road, she was thoroughly exhausted. Her thighs felt like lead, and although at first her trip had seemed so promising, she now doubted the wisdom of it. Breathless, she paused at a store and bought a soda. How was she ever going to make it home? Why had she been so stupid?

Drinking her Coke, she wondered what she would do if she was wrong. This was the right road, but maybe Nicole wasn't even here now.

"There's only one way to find out," Mollie said out loud as she swung her aching leg back over the seat.

Gritting her teeth, she pedaled the last few blocks of her journey.

Whoever this guy was, Mollie had to say she was impressed with his house. From just peering over the hedges, she could see the gardens were enormous and the house itself was almost a mansion. Even though it was in the same Spanish ranch style as the Lewises', it seemed at least ten times as large.

Resting her bike near the gate, Mollie realized she couldn't even get in. She hadn't planned on the front entrance being locked like this. In fact, she hadn't planned very far ahead. But what was she going to do—ring the bell and demand to see Nicole? That would certainly get her into trouble.

She partially hid her bike in some bushes and walked around the edges of the property as she tried to see into the courtyard. If Nicole was there ... but Mollie couldn't see anything over the bushes. Why was she so short? Or so unathletic? If she were Cindy she could probably vault over the fence.

The sound of a honking horn made her run back to the entrance. Someone was going in through the front gate. That meant she could sneak in, too, if she was careful.

Almost without thinking, Mollie forged ahead— only to stop short a few feet from the entrance. The yellow Volvo looked familiar, and in an instant Mollie realized that the person driving it was Nicole!

Paralyzed, Mollie just stood there. She found it hard to believe that she had made it here before her sister—unless, of course, Nicole had been somewhere else, too. Now Mollie wondered where she had gone first.

It took all of Mollie's wits to pull herself into the bushes near the gate before her sister saw her, and then to quickly duck down and follow the car in as the gates closed. Before Nicole could leave the car, Mollie had taken cover under the trees in the front yard.

Breathless, she waited and watched as her older sister got out of her car and walked up the front steps.

The pepper-haired gentleman who answered the door reminded Mollie of Peter Graves from the reruns of *Mission Impossible.* But, of course, it wasn't him. Even so, he looked like the perfect spy.

"Bonjour, ma petite," the man said as he kissed Nicole on both cheeks. "Are you ready?"

Well, so what if he spoke with a French accent? Mollie thought; he could still be a Russian agent. They would, of course, know that Nicole was hopelessly in love with France and use a Frenchman to lure her into their trap.

"Bonjour, Alain." Nicole started into the house almost as if she knew the place.

For the first time since beginning this adventure, Mollie applauded her own quick wit as she pulled out her camera and snapped a couple of Polaroid pictures. Thank goodness she was far enough away so that the noise couldn't be heard.

The initial picture wasn't very good, because all it showed was Nicole's back, but the second photo caught the man full-faced just as the door was closing.

Mollie stared at the shut door and then at the shut gate. Now she had to wait for someone to open the gate so that she could escape, but considering the way her legs were feeling at the moment, it was probably just as well. Resting against one of the trees, Mollie wiped the leaves and twigs off her pants and leaned back and waited.

Her chance came about an hour later, when what appeared to be the maid emerged from the house and climbed into a blue station wagon. Just before the gates closed behind the car, Mollie dashed out.

The beach was unusually crowded for so early on a Saturday morning at this time of year. That's probably, Cindy thought, because the tides are so good today.

Frowning, she parked and locked her bike as she looked around for Bitsy. Grabbing her surfboard and her towels, Cindy headed down toward the section of the beach where the surfers hung out. She knew she'd find her friends there, and Bitsy would just have to find her.

Stepping onto the hot sand, she felt the rays of the sun on her back. It was glorious. She forgot all about Nicole as she watched the waves crashing onto the shore. It was a super day for surfing. She spotted Duffy and Grant, already out on their boards.

Grant waved and motioned her out. But Cindy shook her head and turned around.

"Hey, Cindy! Over here!" Bitsy waved frantically as she attracted Cindy's attention. "I have a great spot right by the lifeguard," Bitsy said in a low voice as she ran up to her friend's sister.

"Why do we need to be by the lifeguard? You can swim," Cindy said scornfully. Her other friends were obviously sleeping late this morning. What a waste of good surf.

Bitsy stared strangely at Cindy. "Because he's gorgeous, that's why." She shook her head. "You know, sometimes I wonder about you. You sure you're Nicole's sister? Even Mollie's more interested in boys than you are." Bitsy giggled, adjusting her bikini strap.

Cindy shrugged. "I never said I didn't like guys. After all, I'm dating Grant."

"Has he asked you to the Alta California Ball yet?"

Cindy shrugged again. "No. I'm not really into dances, though."

Bitsy sighed. "You really are strange. Don't you care about Grant? He might like dances, and I hate to say it, but there are plenty of girls who'd like to go with him."

"Let them, then." Cindy put on her sunglasses to shield her eyes, affecting a lack of concern.

Bitsy only stared at her. Finally, as they neared the spot where Bitsy had staked a claim for them, she said, "I'm sure he's going to ask you, Cindy. Just keep an eye on Susan Hawkins—I think she's after Grant."

Shrugging her shoulders, Cindy didn't reply. A frown crossed her face as she sat down and began to take things out of her bag. As always, she coated her nose with white sunblock. "Bitsy, would you help me put this on my back?"

But there was no answer.

"Bitsy?" Cindy turned around to see Nicole's friend talking to the lifeguard as if he were some sort of demigod. Cindy frowned.

"I'll help you."

As she looked over her shoulder, Cindy saw a dark-haired guy she had never seen before, hovering over her.

"I said I'd help you." He held out his hand for Cindy to give him the bottle of sunblock.

Silently, she handed it up to him.

"You're Cindy Lewis, aren't you?"

"That's right. Who are you?"

He had finished rubbing the lotion on her back. "Rafael Martin." Smiling at her, he handed back the tube and left.

"Was that who I think it was?" Bitsy hurried back to the blanket, breathless with excitement.

"I don't know. Who did you think it was?"

Bitsy was still staring into the crowd "The new football player, Rafael Martin. He's only the handsomest guy on the team."

"Oh."

Bitsy was incredulous. "A man like Rafael Martin stops to talk to you—no, to put suntan lotion on your back—and all you say is 'oh'?" Bitsy shook her head. "No wonder Nicole's flipped over. You're a lost cause."

"I don't think so." Cindy picked up her surfing board. "Now. You do want me to teach you something? Or do you want to gape at these guys all day like some love starved bird?"

"Teach me," Bitsy said. But even as she picked up her surfboard, she smiled up at the lifeguard.

"It's going to be a bit tricky in that bikini," Cindy commented, smoothing down her own red tank suit.

Anna and Carey had joined them within the hour, and soon so did Louise, Bitsy's younger sister. Even Anna knew about Rafael Martin and told Cindy that if she could hook him as a date for the dance, she would really make Grant jealous.

Fortunately, Duffy came over and rescued her from boy talk. After taking their boards out, she and Duffy spent most of the afternoon riding the waves. It had turned out that Bitsy wasn't keen on learning how to surf.

As the girls rested on the blankets again later that day, Bitsy finally asked, "So have you found out why Nicole's been avoiding me?"

Cindy shook her head. "All I know is that she runs to the phone every time it rings, and that girl, the one who calls herself Gabriella, called to say that Nicole's missed the past few meetings of French Club."

"Tell me about it." Bitsy sighed, obviously depressed. "It's like she's become someone totally different, like someone's cast a spell over her."

Cindy just sighed. "You're worse than Mollie. She thinks that Nicole is now working as a spy for the Russians."

Bitsy laughed. "Now that's a bit too far!"

"Of course it is. That's Mollie's theory, but then she's got a wild imagination. Not as wild as yours, though."

"Well, what do you think it really is?"

"I don't know. All I know are the facts I've told you."

"You have to admit, it's strange. She's missing all her activities. She's acting weird toward you guys. She's not sharing with me. Cindy, you know how close we've been. I mean, I bet she told me things she never told you or Mollie."

"Yeah, I bet she has. In fact, you'd probably have a better chance of pinning her down on this. Why don't you ask her something?"

Bitsy made a face. "As if I could. You know as well as I do that Nicole practically runs the other way when she sees me." Bitsy laughed. "Sometimes I wonder if I've developed BO and don't know it."

Cindy was silent.

"You're not saying anything," Bitsy accused her.

"I'm not saying anything because you're being ridiculous."

"Then why is Nicole avoiding me? Why isn't she talking to me?"

"I know why."

Both girls turned to see Mollie standing over them with a big smile on her face, waving several photos in her hand.

Chapter 6

"*What do you mean, you know why?*" Cindy stared at her younger sister.

"Yeah, what's Nicole up to?" Bitsy leaped up as she tried to grab the pictures from Mollie.

Mollie pulled them away quickly with a slight smile. "I was right, Cin." She dropped down beside them onto the blanket. "Nicole's mixed up in something strange. I mean I was there at this huge, huge mansion with acres and acres of land. It's like a palace. All protected with guards, dogs, just like those spies you see on TV."

"Where?" Cindy's eyes narrowed.

"Montecito, I guess. At least I think so, according to the address." She rubbed her aching thighs. "I overheard her talking to someone...."

"Mollie, you'd better start at the beginning. You're losing me. Nicole left the house before me this morning. How do you know where she went? Where did you overhear her?"

Mollie shrugged and flushed. "Well." She glanced around to make sure that no one else was about except her immediate friends.

"The mail came just before I left and there was a letter for Nicole from Marcella."

"So? What's so unusual about that?" Bitsy asked. "Marcella and Nicole write all the time. Not that she wrote me once when I was a junior counselor last summer at Fairchild camp, but who's counting."

"Well, I thought it might be something. I mean, she has been talking in French a lot lately. I thought maybe it was part of their code."

Cindy just shook her head. "Hurry up and get on with your story."

Mollie gulped some soda from Cindy's can and related to her sister and friends how she had hidden in the closet, and then how she had rubbed the paper—just like they did on TV. And then how she had gone on her bike to the address, arriving just when Nicole came in.

"And this is her contact." With a flourish, she handed her sister the pictures. "Now do you believe me?"

"Wait a sec," Bitsy stared over Cindy's shoulder. "I know that guy."

"How would you know someone like him? He's gorgeous!" Louise asked.

Bitsy gave her sister a cross-eyed look. "I mean I've seen him before—with Nicole."

"You have?" It was Cindy's turn to be surprised and Mollie's turn to gloat.

"Yeah. A few days ago. I saw them having coffee at the new shop in town. I started to go up to Nicole because I wanted to talk to her, and suddenly she stood up and left with the guy."

"Did she see you?" Anna asked.

Bitsy shrugged. "I don't know. All I know is that he was acting awfully strange, and so was she."

Cindy took the photos again and looked at them. Whatever Nicole was into—and Cindy still didn't believe Mollie's theory—they had to find out.

Later, alone with her younger sister, Cindy asked, "What else did Nicole say when you talked to her the other night? I mean, it sounds as if you were leading the conversation."

Mollie was wide-eyed. "I wouldn't do that. Honestly, she said she planned to visit Russia." She paused. "At least I think that's what she said."

"Come on, Mol, think about something else." Cindy dipped her finger into the gooey fudge batter for the brownies she was making. "There

SECRETS AT SEVENTEEN   63

must have been something else that would give
us a clue."

Mollie stuck her finger in the bowl as Cindy
pushed her hand away. "We were talking about
guys and about Steve and Mark. She said that not
all guys were mature and she preferred someone
older."

"Did she really say that?"

"I think so," Mollie looked doubtful.

Cindy paused with the bowl in midair. "Do you
think she's ... dating this man?"

It was Mollie's turn to be surprised. "But why
wouldn't she tell us? Why wouldn't she have him
come around? Mark practically lived here when
they were dating."

"Right. But Mark's in high school. If this guy
you took the photo of is the one she's dating ..."
Cindy wiped her hands on her jeans, and grabbed
for the photos again. "I mean, he is awfully old.
Maybe she knew Mom and Dad wouldn't approve."

Mollie shook her head. "Naw. She'd have told
us, at least. Or even Bitsy." Mollie sighed and
managed to sneak a fingerful of fudge as she
headed out the door.

"Where are you going?"

"Just riding."

"I thought you had enough riding for today. At
least that's what you told Mom on the phone. You
said you were so exhausted you couldn't even
climb the stairs to clean your room."

"That was an hour ago." Mollie smiled. "Steve and his friends usually hang out at Taco Rio at about this time. I thought I'd wander down there and get a Coke."

Cindy made a face. "You're making a mistake, spending all your time chasing after boys. It won't get you anywhere."

"You should talk," Mollie snorted.

"What does that mean?"

"You haven't hooked Grant yet. He hasn't asked you to the dance. And you don't even know how to flirt properly with a guy like Rafael Martin. What a waste. I think you should have been the youngest, not me."

Before Cindy could retort, Mollie had slammed the door and ridden off.

In her room later, feet tucked under her and a plate of hot brownies in front of her, Cindy attempted to get Anna and Carey to work on their history papers, rather than talk about boys and the upcoming dance.

"Do you think Grant's going to ask you?" Anna asked for probably the fourth time that hour.

"I bet if he doesn't, Rafael Martin will," Carey sighed. "I don't know how you do it, Cindy. Two beautiful guys, and you don't even care."

"You're right. I don't care." Cindy eyed the plate of brownies. She'd already had three, but she picked up her fourth and took an enormous bite.

"What if they *both* ask you?" Anna giggled.

Cindy shrugged, pretending she was busy chewing.

"I wish I had your problem. All I know is Sam had better ask me, or ..."

"Or what?" Carey laughed. "Will you kill him?"

Anna shook her head and wrapped her long brown hair around her pinkie. "Maybe I'll ask him, instead."

"You wouldn't dare!" Carey was aghast.

"Why not?" Cindy stood up for Anna this time. "If she really wants to go, there's no reason why she shouldn't ask him. What's the big deal?"

Carey sighed. "I don't even have anyone to ask. But even so, I don't think it's right. After all, the party is being given by Alpha Sigma. The guys should do the asking."

"Well, I'm doing some asking now," Cindy interrupted. "I want to work on our medieval history. You did come over to study for the exam, didn't you?"

Anna frowned. "Yeah, but we have all day. And since when did you become so interested in homework?" Changing the subject, she glanced toward Cindy's open closet. "You'll have to get your mom to buy you a new dress." She unfolded her long legs and picked up one of the eye shadows Nicole had given Cindy. Without asking, Anna tried it on.

After all, Cindy would probably never use it. Why let it go to waste?

"Anna, if she decides to go, that's the least of her problems. I think you look better with the green," Carey said, pointing toward the other shadow on the neat, never-used makeup tray. "I hear that dance sometimes gets a little wild."

Cindy swallowed the last of another brownie and turned to Anna. "What is she talking about?"

Anna flushed and shrugged uncomfortably. "She means that since it's not held at school and there aren't any chaperones, the dance floor is sometimes pretty empty."

"Oh." The four brownies now sat like a lump in Cindy's stomach. "Grant wouldn't ... I mean ... he ..." She was becoming too flustered to think. "Look, right now, I doubt that I'm going to the Alta California Ball with Grant or anyone else. I don't like dances anyway."

"Do you want to bet he'll still ask you?"

"Even after he finds out about the lead balls I put in his tennis bag?" Cindy couldn't keep her secret.

Anna's eyes opened wide. "When'd you do that?"

"Yesterday. When he wasn't looking. After I win the next set, he'll learn a thing or two about losing."

Carey took a dollar out of her wallet. "I still bet.

That guy has the hots for you, Cindy. At least that's what I hear."

"Who told you that? Mollie?" Cindy flushed again as Anna covered Carey's bet. Her feelings right now were so mixed up. She liked Grant, but she didn't like dances. Actually, she'd never gone to one, but she knew she wouldn't like it. Mollie was right; she didn't know how to flirt or act feminine or like a girl at all—so how was she supposed to act at a formal dance? But if he didn't at least ask her . . .

"Okay, if he asks me to the dance in spite of everything, and I go with him, then I owe you guys two history papers!"

It was Carey's turn to be wide-eyed. "Are you serious? I mean, I hate history and all, but . . ."

"I'm serious."

"That's not much of a bet," Anna commented, taking the last of the brownies. "You're not doing so well in history, Cin."

"Then maybe we better think about history for a change, and forget boys."

Anna, Carey, and Cindy met in front of the gym the following day. "He say anything yet?"

"Nope," Cindy responded to Anna's question. "But I am playing tennis with him later."

"I think I'll drop by. I can't wait to see his face when he tries to serve," Carey laughed. "Still, he's going to ask you. At least that's what the rumor mill says."

"He can ask, but I still don't think I'll go."

"And we still think you're crazy."

Cindy checked her watch. "I've got Spanish now. I don't know why we even have to take a language. It's not like I plan to visit Spain." She sighed, "Oh, well. Wish me luck on the exam. See you guys later."

In her own advanced French class, Nicole wasn't doing very well.

"Nicole, please translate the question I just asked the class, and answer the question."

Nicole continued to draw on her pad.

"Nicole ..."

Bitsy nudged Nicole.

She looked up to find the whole class watching her. "Did you want something, Madame Preston?" Nicole tried to put a smile on her face.

"I asked you to translate for the class what I just said."

"Oh." Nicole glanced at Bitsy. But her friend couldn't help her here. "I'm sorry, Madame Preston. My mind was on other things. I ..."

"Yes, I can see." Madame Preston repeated the phrase, and Nicole quickly gave the proper French response and then replied in English as well.

"Nicole, you'll see me after class."

"But I ..." She paused, realizing that she was

making a fool of herself. "Yes, Madame Preston." Nicole knew she had responded correctly. Obviously, her French teacher was upset at her daydreaming. Well, others did it. Why couldn't she, once in a while? She sighed. She'd just have to take Madame Preston into her confidence. Once her teacher saw how very important this afternoon was, Nicole was sure she would excuse her absentmindedness.

Bitsy cornered Cindy later in the hall. "I saw the name."

"What name?"

"The name that Mollie told us the other day. Alain. She was drawing it on her French notes when Madame Preston called on her. If it hadn't been for me . . ."

"Did you ask her anything about him?"

Bitsy shook her head. "I couldn't. She had to stay late because she missed the question, and then she ran off to her next class before I could."

Cindy frowned. "I'll try to ask her tonight. Knowing Nicole, though, she'll find some way to avoid me. Right now I've got to get to tennis."

"Oh, yeah. With Grant."

Cindy stared at the other girl. "How did you know?"

"Well, everyone knows that he's going to ask you to the dance today. I guess it'll be while you're playing."

Cindy clenched her fists. She knew Grant would

never have started a rumor like that. He was a private person, like she was. Why was everyone in this school so nosy? She wished everyone would just stay out of her affairs.

Chapter 7

*M*ollie slid onto the bench seat next to Steve
at Taco Rio. Somehow she was going to get him to
ask her to the Alta California dance—today. It
had to be today. If Steve didn't ask now, she'd
never have enough time to get a new dress.

"Hi!" She smiled at him as she helped herself to
one of his nacho chips and dipped it into the
gooey cheese.

"Hi," he acknowledged as he moved the chip
basket closer to him. The waitress came over.

"What'll you have?"

"Uh," Mollie glanced at Steve. He was drinking
a Coke. She'd have the same.

"Sure you don't want some chips, too?" Steve
asked as Mollie gave her order.

"Can't." Mollie pressed her lips together. "My allowance . . ."

She was elated when he took the bait. "Go ahead," he told the waitress. "Bring us another basket of chips. I'll pay."

"Thanks." Mollie gave him a generous smile. "That was really sweet of you."

Steve shrugged and laughed. "If I hadn't, you'd have eaten all of mine. Anyway, I probably would have ordered a second basket later. Mom's got a late meeting at work, so this is dinner."

"Lucky you. When our mother has to work late, we always have to *make* dinner."

"Tough. But I can't even boil water, so Mom gives me money to eat out."

Mollie stared at him. She had never heard of anyone being so helpless that they couldn't boil water! Of course, she'd almost set the kitchen on fire once, trying to scramble eggs. . . .

"How's the math coming?"

"Okay. But I wanted to ask you—" Mollie suddenly blanked out. She couldn't just ask him to take her to the party. She had to make him ask her.

"Ask me what?" He took a long sip of soda and flipped through the pages of his biology book, not really paying attention to her.

Mollie reached over, accidentally on purpose spilling a few of the chips onto his book. "Oh, I'm sorry." She fluttered her lashes, feeling desperate now.

"Mollie, what did you want to ask me?" He watched as the waitress put down her Coke and the extra basket of chips.

Pretending to be hungry, she scooped up more cheese sauce onto one of the chips.

"Mollie, I don't have time to tutor you in math. So if you were going to ask it, I'm sorry."

"Oh." She flushed, realizing he had given her the perfect excuse out. "Then I guess I shouldn't even have brought up the subject." As if she had! "You're right, Steve. I was going to ask if you could help me with my math—uh, next Friday night."

Steve drained his Coke with a loud slurping sound that made her wince. "Next Friday night? That's the Alta California Ball." He shook his head. "Sorry, even if I had the time, I couldn't."

"Oh." She looked down at her books, drinking her soda and pretending to be upset. Actually, it wasn't much of a pretense. She was upset—but not about math.

What else was she going to say? How else could she get across that she wanted him to invite her?

"Listen," he said as Mollie took another handful of chips. "Listen, I really have a lot of studying to do, Mollie."

Mollie's mouth hung open for a fraction of a second—cheese, chips, and all. "But I . . ."

It was no use. He had already turned his attention to the biology book. Jeez!

"Yeah, sure." She grabbed her soda, the basket of chips, and moved over to the table where her friends Linda and Sarah were waiting and watching.

"What a creep!" Mollie took the seat next to Linda. "I'm just as glad he didn't ask me." She sipped her soda, forgetting that this time Steve had at least bought her the drink. "I hope Cindy's doing better than I am."

On the courts outside the school, Cindy had just served for the fourth time.

"You're not doing so well today, Grant." She smiled at him. "Could it be that I'm actually getting better than you?"

"Impossible," he grumbled. "Something's wrong with the racquet. I'm changing to my second one."

"Sure. Why don't you just admit, though, that just because you're a guy doesn't mean you're going to be best?"

"I never said that."

Cindy hit the ball smack into middle court. She was almost glad that he was able to return it. "It sure seemed like that the other day."

"Cindy, can't we forget that? Look, I don't want to upset you. I just want us to . . ." He paused long enough to return the ball again.

She moved swiftly to the other side of the court.

"Cindy, if no one's asked you to the Alto California Ball yet, I'd like you to go with me."

The yellow tennis ball landed at her feet. She had been afraid he wouldn't ask her.

"Well?"

"It's your serve," she responded.

"But what about the dance?"

"Serve first." She tried to keep herself calm as the emotions flooded over her like a rough wave.

Grant shrugged and picked up one of his balls. It landed at his feet.

"I can't understand that. It's the third time." He picked up the ball again. "Wait a minute. This seems awfully heavy...." He glanced at Cindy, an expression of suspicion on his face.

"Serves you right, thinking your serve is always the best." She stood at the net waiting for him to comment.

He looked at her and then at the tennis bag. Suddenly, he burst out laughing. "Guess you're right. It does serve me." Grant picked up his racquet again. "So? What about Friday night?" He crossed the court and put his arm around her.

Cindy felt a strange warmth go through her, and she could only stare at him. She wanted to say yes, but she was having trouble finding the right words. Instead, she blurted out, "Are you sure no one put you up to this?"

Grant looked at her questioningly. "Put me up to it? Cindy, do you think I would be influenced by anyone else?" He leaned over and kissed her. "So?"

Flushed, Cindy glanced around quickly to make sure no one had seen. "Of course I'll go."

Bitsy was shocked to find Nicole sitting alone in Pete's Pizzeria.

"Someone stand you up?"

"What?" Nicole looked up from her notebook. "Oh, hi, Bitsy. Sit down." Nicole was trying to be friendly.

"Someone named Alain supposed to meet you— or something?" Bitsy remained standing.

"What do you know about Alain?" Nicole's eyes narrowed as she assessed her friend.

"Only that you had his name written all over your French book and seemed so lost in thought about him that you couldn't answer Madame Preston today."

"Oh. That." Nicole seemed relieved.

"Yes. That." Bitsy sat down and started to take a handful of fries from Nicole's basket and then recalled the diet she was supposed to be on. If she wasn't careful, she'd never fit into her dress for the Alta California dance. "Come on, Nicole," she pleaded. "Who is he? I know he doesn't go to Vista. How old is he? Where'd you meet him? How long have you known him?"

"Bitsy, it's not what you think." Nicole responded warily to the barrage of questions.

"Then tell me."

Nicole merely munched on a french fry.

"Come on. Please. I tell you everything."

"He's just a friend and he's helping me with a project. That's all I'm going to say about it, now."

Frustrated, Bitsy stood up to leave.

"I'm sorry, Bitsy. I promise I'll tell you when I'm ready. I just can't yet. Not now."

Nicole gave Bitsy a reassuring squeeze of the hand and then left the restaurant before her disappointed friend could convince her to talk.

"Jeez!" Bitsy cursed as she picked up one of the fries from the basket that Nicole had left behind. Diet or no diet, it was silly to let good food go to waste.

"Well, what did you say?" Anna was breathless with excitement as Cindy related the events of the afternoon.

Cindy put a finger to her lip, tiptoed across the room, and opened the bedroom door. Mollie practically fell in.

"Well, I want to know what you said, too. I mean, it affects my whole life." Mollie defended herself against her sister's accusing look.

"Melodramatic Mollie!" Cindy laughed at her sister.

"It's true. First Nicole tells me that she's going

with Rafael Martin, and now you're going with Grant. Who's left for me?" Her hand went to her brow. "I don't think I'll ever recover from being left out."

"You'll recover. I'm sure you'll go next year."

"The question is, are you going this year?" Carey put in her two cents.

Cindy shrugged. "I said yes."

"All right!" Carey screeched. "Do my paper on Richard the Lionhearted."

Cindy made a face. "Well, maybe ..."

"Don't you dare think it!" Anna sat her friend down in front of the makeup mirror, which Cindy never used. "If you're going depends on not doing our papers, then you can forget the papers. We're not letting you get out of this."

"No, I don't suppose you would," Cindy laughed.

Anna patted her friend's shoulder. "Now we have to figure out what you're going to wear and what to do with this hair," Anna grabbed a handful of Cindy's short sun-bleached hair.

"Leave my hair alone!" Cindy screeched.

"Look, if you don't want our advice you can always ask Nicole. She always looks absolutely perfect."

"Yeah. Right. If I can get her to talk to me these days."

Carey got out the makeup tray as she turned up the radio. "Shall we practice?"

"Oh, why not? Practice makes perfect in sports. I guess it's the same for putting on makeup."

Cindy waited up that night, hoping to catch Nicole when she came in. But her older sister hadn't come home yet, and it was nearly eleven-thirty. She was surprised that Mom and Dad weren't worried.

"Is Nicole all right?" Cindy finally asked her mom.

"Yes, dear. She called from Bitsy's. She'll be home shortly."

There was nothing Cindy could say without blowing her sister's cover, but she was sure that Nicole was not at Bitsy's. She only wished that she knew where Nicole was and what was really happening with her.

She thought about the recent turn of events. If Nicole was going to the dance with Rafael, then maybe this guy Alain really was just a friend. But that still didn't explain Nicole's mysterious disappearances. If Alain was just a friend, why was she hiding him?

In the hall light, she stared at the photo of Alain. He was just the kind of man Nicole would find attractive.

Downstairs, she heard the door slam. Her sister was home—but Cindy heard the door to Nicole's room close. She obviously wouldn't get her answers tonight.

Chapter 8

*T*he next few days seemed to fly by. Here Cindy was seated at her makeup table with Anna and Carey as she practiced for this evening's dance.

She had to admit, she was still rather worried about the whole thing. None of her close friends were going. She was the only one not excited about the dance, and here she was getting ready for it. Staring at her reflection in the mirror, she hardly recognized herself. All that makeup looked odd on her face, she thought. And how was she supposed to dance in a long dress? Well, at least Nicole would be there. She'd just watch Nicole and imitate her. She could count on Nicole to behave perfectly.

Cindy had been surprised that Nicole seemed

to be back to normal the last few days. Even Bitsy had commented that her friend acted as if nothing had ever happened—and yet there was still something going on. Cindy was sure of it, and so was Mollie.

On the night of the party, Mollie sat on Cindy's bed while her older sister dressed. Nicole had already left with Rafael about an hour earlier, since he was on the planning committee and had to help set up.

"You look absolutely great, Cindy," Mollie sighed. "I wish I was going, too."

Cindy shrugged. She didn't know if she was glad or not. She supposed she was, and yet—

"What's that!" Cindy sat up straight as they heard the slamming of brakes outside and then the squeal of burning rubber on the street.

"Probably some of the guys playing with their cars."

"Probably," Cindy responded, feeling something cold in the pit of her stomach. She adjusted the sash on the Mexican embroidered dress that she had decided to wear tonight. She could have gotten her mother to buy her something new—as Anna had urged her to do—but what was the use? She didn't wear dresses all that often, and it was silly to waste the money when she'd rather have a new surfboard or more scuba gear.

All of a sudden they heard Winston barking outside. Getting up from the table and peering out the window, Cindy watched Winnie running back and forth across the lawn.

"Mol," Cindy asked, "go out and check on Winston. He seems anxious."

"He's always anxious to get in." Mollie continued to lounge on the bed. "Where'd Mom go?"

"She and Dad went out to dinner. You know that." Cindy continued to struggle with the makeup as the dog barked outside.

"All right," Mollie told the dog, reluctantly moving from her comfortable position on the bed. "Use the purple shadows," she said as she went out. "I read an article in *Seventeen* that says purple eye shadow makes your green eyes look greener."

"Right." Cindy stared at the array of makeup pots before her. It didn't make sense. Why did she have to use anything at all? Guys didn't wear makeup.

She started to smile, imagining how strange Grant or Duffy would look with lipstick and eyeshadow.

"Cin! Cin! Come quick!"

The tone of Mollie's voice left no moment for question. Dropping a liner pencil, Cindy rushed to the hall and down the stairs.

"Cindy, it's ..." Mollie was choking on her words, and tears rolled down her face.

Without questioning her sister, Cindy lifted the long skirts of her Mexican dress and ran outside.

Almost immediately she saw Cinders lying on the side of the road. "Oh, Cinders. Oh, baby." Cindy sniffled back her tears and told herself to be calm. The cat was still alive, and if she could help, Cinders would remain so.

"Get me a towel," she told Mollie. "Quickly."

Mollie continued to stare.

"Quickly, Mollie! We can still save her, I think."

Finally, Mollie ran back into the house to obey her sister, but only after Cindy had already taken off her embroidered shawl. Mom would have a fit, but she couldn't think about that now. Cinders was the only thing to worry about now.

"It's okay, baby," Cindy spoke softly to the cat. "I'll take care of you." As she wrapped her shawl around the injured animal, blood seeped through, and Cindy struggled with her own fear and panic.

Damn that driver! Why hadn't he stopped? Why hadn't he rung the bell, at least, to let someone know Cinders had been hurt? After all, she had a tag on.

"It's all right, Cinders." She kept on stroking the cat as Mollie came out of the house carrying a towel.

"What are you going to do?"

"Do?" Cindy questioned as she wrapped the towel tightly around the cat, trying to prevent shock. "I'm taking her to the vet's. Now."

"But you can't drive. You don't have a license."

"I've got my student license, and I've driven a couple of times with Dad."

"But you—"

"Shut up, Mollie. They'll understand. Hurry up. Get me the keys," Cindy ordered her sister.

Mollie hesitated.

"Now! Unless you want Cinders to die right here."

Just as Mollie came out with the keys, Grant pulled up in his red Trans Am. "Hey, you're not ready? What's that bundle you have? A present for me?"

Cindy shook her head as she practically ran to the car. "Cinders got hit by a car. I'm taking her to the vet."

"But the dance! Can't Mollie take him? We—"

"Her? No, Mollie can't. My cat is dying, Grant. *I'm* taking her to the vet. If everything is all right, I'll meet you at the dance later."

"Wait a sec." He got out of the car and headed her off. "You can't drive."

"I can. I have my student license. Look, I've already had this argument with Mollie. Every second we waste here, Cinders is dying. If you don't want me to drive, then you drive me."

Grant stared at her a moment. "I can't. I'm supposed to be there at—"

"Fine. Then move out of my way." Cindy interrupted him and hurried toward her mother's car.

"Wait. Wait, I'll take you." Grant opened the car door.

Cindy nodded and ran toward Grant's car. "The vet's in the shopping mall. He's got a twenty-four-hour service, and Mollie's already called him."

"Right." Grant revved the motor, and Cindy had to clutch the dashboard to keep from jarring the injured cat.

"It's all right, Cinders, baby. It's all right. We're going to get you help." Tears were in her eyes as she stroked the cheek of the cat. Cinders had closed her eyes, and Cindy prayed it wasn't too late.

Cindy paced the vet's waiting room. She wished that Grant had waited for her, but he said he had to go ahead to the dance, so he'd left. She was glad he had driven her, because student driver or not, she knew she would have had trouble trying to drive and comfort Cinders at the same time. Nevertheless, he could have been a bit more gracious about it. He hadn't understood why she couldn't just leave Cinders at the vet's and go to the dance.

Imagine! Being more concerned about a dance than a cat!

Cindy sucked in her lower lip. How could she even think about caring for someone who thought her silly for putting so much affection and worry into an animal. How could she like someone who thought a dance was more important than a life?

She continued to pace until finally the vet came out.

"Is she going to be all right?"

Dr. Osgood nodded. "Yes. She lost a lot of blood and we had to give her a transfusion, but her injuries weren't as bad as I suspected. We're keeping her overnight to make sure she's stable. And she'll have a few days of antibiotics as well as something to keep her quiet and in the house. But she should make it just fine. A real fighter, that one."

"Thank you, doctor."

"It's you she has to thank. If you hadn't thought to wrap her up warmly, she might have died of shock." He shook his head. "I can't understand these drivers who hit an animal and then don't stop."

"Neither do I." Cindy picked up her bloodied shawl and then decided to wrap it into the plastic. She'd have to take it to the cleaners tomorrow. "I'll be back tomorrow with my mom to pay for her and pick her up."

"You're walking home? What happened to your ride?"

Cindy pressed her lips together. "He's gone."

"Well, be careful. I'd drive you myself, but I have to stay with the animals."

Cindy smiled at him. "It's all right. It's not far."

She started out the door and down the dark street, shivering in the cold night air. It would have been nice if she had something to cover herself with, but Cinders had been more important, and Cindy didn't regret anything—except maybe Grant's reaction.

The honking of the horn startled her. She stopped as Grant's car pulled up.

"Get in."

"I thought you were at the dance."

He made a face. "I was. But I couldn't enjoy myself thinking about you back here, and when I stopped at the vet's, he told me you had started to walk."

"Yeah." Cindy got into the car next to him, relieved to be warm again and glad that Grant had come back for her. "She's going to be okay."

"The vet told me. I'm glad."

"So am I."

They reached the Lewises' home a few moments later. "Do you want to clean up and come back to the dance with me?" His voice had a wistful tone to it that she found hard to ignore. And for the first time that night she noticed how handsome he looked in a blue jacket and yellow tie. It also made him look a lot older and more sophisticated. Suddenly she felt like an immature kid.

Cindy thought for just a moment and then shook her head. "I don't think I'm in the mood for a dance, not with Cinders in the hospital."

Grant smiled, displaying a dimple. "C'mon, Cindy. You can't do anything for the cat now. Let's have some fun."

"I'm sorry. I just don't feel like having fun."

"That's obvious." Grant frowned. "I don't think you even wanted to go in the first place."

Cindy narrowed her eyes a moment. "You just don't understand anything." She got out of the car and slammed the door.

"Wait!" Grant left the car and went after her. "Look, I'm sorry about that remark. You're right. I don't understand. I've never had a pet, so I guess it's hard for me to understand why you're still so upset."

"Yes." Cindy pulled her arm away from his. "I guess it is."

"Cindy, I'm trying to apologize. Please. Come back to the dance with me?"

Cindy shook her head. "Sorry, not tonight, Grant. Too many things have happened, and I want to think. Besides, Mollie's all alone."

"She's a big girl. She can take care of herself. In fact"—he opened the door, and the noise of Mollie's stereo echoed throughout the house—"I guess she's doing fine."

Cindy shrugged. She was just too tired and too confused. "Good night, Grant. I'm sorry for ruining your evening. But I really don't feel like dancing tonight. Next time, okay?"

"Sure." He sighed and took her hand for a brief moment. "Next time."

Cindy watched as he returned to his car and pulled out of the driveway. Maybe she had lost Grant forever, but she couldn't help it.

As she entered the house, she picked up Smokey to comfort and cuddle him. "Yes, baby, Cinders is going to be all right."

Smokey laid his head on Cindy's shoulder, his paw on her neck, and somehow she knew that the cat understood.

Chapter 9

*B*y Sunday Cinders *was back in the house and,* except for a few stitches, was as feisty as ever. Everyone else seemed to have recovered from Friday night, too. Everyone but Mollie, who still felt cheated that she hadn't gone to the dance, and while she loved Cinders, too, she thought Cindy was stupid for not having gone with Grant.

To make matters worse, she'd heard that Steve had been one of the few guys at the party without a date. Now, why couldn't he have asked her? It just wasn't fair.

Sipping a soda at Taco Rio, Mollie chatted with Linda and Sarah but kept one eye on the door, hoping that Steve would come in. Maybe if she played up to one of the other boys when he was around, Steve would get jealous and would see what he was missing. After all, one dance was over, but there was still the Sadie Hawkins party in two weeks.

And for that dance, *she* would ask him. But she didn't want to unless he showed a *little* more interest in her.

"Can you believe what Jan Armant's older sister did?" Linda's voice was hushed with awe. "It's unbelievable."

"What?" Mollie asked, always eager for gossip. She bit into the taco, and vegetables oozed out, along with cheese and chili sauce.

"Mollie doesn't want to know." Sarah smiled. "I already heard, and it's not worth knowing."

"C'mon, you guys. Tell me. I can't stand having secrets kept from me. You know it."

"Really, Mol, it's nothing," Sarah teased. "Besides, poor Jan probably doesn't want the worst blabbermouth in school knowing it."

"I am not a blabbermouth!" Mollie pushed Sarah playfully. "Come on. Tell me." She grabbed some of Linda's nacho chips and threatened to drop them into her soda.

"Okay. Okay." Linda leaned closer and whispered. "Jan's sister ran away with a sailor who's ten years older than her!"

"She married him?"

Linda shrugged. "That's what Jan thinks."

"You mean, she ran away without telling her family anything? Didn't they suspect?"

Sarah shook her head. "Jan says her sister was never around and no one had any idea she was even seeing this guy."

Mollie nearly gagged on her taco. "You don't think ... Nicole ...!" She stared out the window. Instead of seeing Steve, as she had hoped, she saw her older sister wearing a straw hat and sunglasses, carrying a large package. Mollie stood up suddenly.

"Where you going, Mollie?"

"I ... uh ... I have to talk to Cindy. Right away. Forgot to tell her something this morning." She grabbed her purse and books and rushed out of the restaurant without paying.

On the street, she paused breathlessly for a moment as she looked around. Where had Nicole disappeared to? Had she already lost her? She just had to follow her. This time they were both on foot, so there was no excuse for Mollie's losing her.

Down the block, she spied her sister hurrying along. Mollie broke into a run and then, as she neared, realized that she had to be a little more discreet. She couldn't let Nicole know she was following her. That would ruin everything.

Slowing down to a fast-paced walk, Mollie tried to stay close to the buildings and out of sight. Out of the corner of her eye, she saw her friend

Heather across the street, motioning frantically to her.

Please don't call out my name, Mollie prayed as she continued to follow Nicole down the street.

Mollie wondered what was in the bulky package. It was obvious from the way Nicole carried it that it was of great value. And why was she dressed like that? Mollie had never seen those clothes before.

She continued to hurry after Nicole as her sister went into the mall. Through the round-about doors and then—nothing.

Mollie stared at the people gathered in the long covered hallways, seated on the cushioned benches near the fountains, lounging in the store entrances. Where was Nicole? She couldn't have lost her. She just couldn't have.

Angry with herself for not having been faster, Mollie cursed and started checking each store. But Nicole was nowhere in sight.

Obviously, her sister had known that she was being followed and had purposely lost her. Maybe she was a spy after all. Depressed, Mollie sat down near one of the fountains and bought a macadamia nut cookie to ease her hurt feelings.

Having just bitten into the sweet, she stood abruptly and jammed the cookie back into the white sack. There was Nicole! She had taken off her hat and was standing next to a guy—it looked like the same guy Mollie had taken a photo of the other day. He was even carrying a package that looked like the one Nicole had had earlier. They had made their transaction already, and Mollie hadn't been there.

"Nicole!" she called out, forgetting that she was supposed to be discreetly following her. "Nicole!"

Her shoulder-length light brown hair swirled across her face as she turned around. It wasn't Nicole!

"Sorry," Mollie mumbled. "I thought you were someone I knew."

The girl shrugged as Mollie sank back down onto the bench to finish her cookie. She shook her head, realizing what a stupid thing she had just done.

"And then what happened?" Cindy questioned.

"Then I lost her."

"You were probably following the wrong girl all along." Cindy paused as she opened the refrigerator door and took out a piece of cold chicken. Biting into a drumstick, she said, "What your friends were telling you about Jan's sister seems to fit the situation a lot better than a spy ring. I mean, I don't think Nicole would do that either, but ..."

"But something's going on. I think we ought to check through her room."

Cindy put down the chicken and grabbed a brownie from the plate on the table. Somehow food helped her think better. "You know she keeps her room locked."

"Jeez, you don't have any imagination, do you?"

"And you have too much," Cindy said as her eyes widened. Mollie had just produced the key to Nicole's room.

"Where did you ...?"

"It's a duplicate." Mollie grinned. "I may not be good at tailing, but they don't call me Mollie the Moll for nothing," she said, imitating a gangster accent. "You game, sweetheart?" She used the key as a cigar and pretended to puff.

Cindy nodded. "Yeah, but let's hurry. Mom will be home soon, and I don't want her catching us."

"Nobody catches the Moll."

Cindy shook her head and laughed as she hurried after her sister.

They were right; the door was locked, but the key fit perfectly.

"Okay, we start with the drawers. That's where I found those tests. I bet there's other things underneath the sweaters."

"And I bet you just want to look at her sweaters."

"Cindy, this is serious."

"Oh, that's right," Cindy replied. "Our sister might be hanged for being a spy."

Mollie merely shook her head and then opened the drawer.

There was nothing there, except sweaters. Even the tests were gone.

"I wonder if they really were tests. Maybe they were part of the secret code."

"Oh, Mol, would you shut up about this spy business? If you say that one more time," Cindy threatened. "I know Nicole isn't involved in anything like that. But I do think ..." Cindy stared at the magazine under the nightgowns. "Since when does Nicole buy *Bride's*? And here's another. *Modern Wedding.*"

"Shhh!" Mollie froze and quickly shut the drawer. "Someone's coming."

"I didn't—"

Mollie clamped her hand over Cindy's mouth as the door to Nicole's room suddenly opened.

"What are you girls doing in here?" Mrs. Lewis said.

"Uh ..." Mollie glanced quickly at Cindy. "It's a surprise ... for Nicole's birthday. We're planning to buy something and we wanted to make sure it would be the right color."

Mrs. Lewis frowned. "Well, I don't think you should be in here without your sister's permission. Besides, I need your help putting away groceries, Cindy."

"Aw, Mom. I've got to study for a test."

"It will only take a minute. You can help, too, Mollie."

Mollie blew out an exasperated sigh. "Yeah, sure."

Mrs. Lewis had already disappeared down the steps. "Now, girls," she called back.

Cindy turned to Mollie. "You think she believed us?"

"Of course," Mollie was confident. She pushed Cindy toward the door. "You go on. I want to have one last look."

Frowning, Cindy went out as Mollie quickly opened the sweater drawer and took out the blue angora sweater. She might as well take advantage of the situation. She was going with Linda and Sarah to the movies tonight, and she had overheard a conversation that Steve would be there, too. If this didn't get him, nothing would.

Mollie hoped that Nicole would pull her usual "Sorry I can't stay for dinner" routine and leave quickly so that she could sneak out of the house in Nicole's sweater. But it didn't work that way. For once, Nicole was eating at home and staying around afterward.

Mollie wanted to get ready and kept looking at the clock, but she didn't want Nicole to see that she had swiped the sweater. Well, swiped wasn't the right word. She was only borrowing it. After all, it looked so good on her. Nicole couldn't be mad—could she?

It was getting late and there was no time to waste. Hoping that she could sneak out of the house without being noticed, Mollie hurried upstairs.

She stood for a moment in front of the mirror, admiring the sweater. Now, if she could only borrow some of Cindy's eyeshadows—

"Just where did you get that!"

Mollie turned to see an angry Nicole staring at her from her open door. She flushed. "I . . . I just wanted to borrow it. You haven't worn it yet."

"That's right, Mollie. *I* haven't worn it yet, and it's mine. Therefore, you shouldn't be the first to wear it."

"But Nicole, it looks so good on me and I want Steve to notice me and . . ." Mollie took a deep breath. "If you don't let me wear it tonight, I'll tell about the tests."

Mollie had expected Nicole to scream at her, but instead, Nicole's face went white. Her voice became softer. "You've been sneaking around in my room." She stared at Mollie and then at the blue sweater. "Fine. Wear it. But if you get it dirty, you're in big trouble."

Mollie's voice was strained as she stared at her sister. "Don't worry. I'll take good care of it, Nicole."

"Yeah, just like you took care of my Yves St. Laurent blouse! And if I ever catch you in my room again—you're turning into a real sneak, Mollie."

Nicole disappeared again, slamming the door to her room behind her, leaving a stunned Mollie.

Nicole must be hiding something really big. She wouldn't care about a couple of tests. And she knew Mollie would never have told her parents. Besides, Mollie had been caught borrowing her sister's things before and she had never reacted like this.

Chapter 10

"So, how's your cat?" Grant leaned against the row of lockers as Cindy put her books away.

"Better."

"It was a great dance. I'm sorry you missed it. Everyone asked about you."

"What'd you say?" Cindy's brow furrowed as she tried to think which notebook she needed for her next class. Why was it that whenever Grant was near she had trouble thinking?

He shrugged and put his arm around her shoulder. "Told them you were taking care of a sick cat." He laughed. "They didn't believe me. Thought you stood me up."

"I wouldn't ... I ... you know."

Grant nodded. "I know, Cindy. But how about

proving it by going with me to the Sadie Hawkins dance next month?"

Cindy pursed her lips. "I thought girls were supposed to ask the guys to Sadie Hawkins."

"They are, but since I knew you wouldn't ask me, I'm asking you." He grinned. "I've legally changed my name to Granella."

Cindy frowned.

"You know—Cordelia, Regan, and Granella."

That was it! Her English book. "You mean Goneril. Even I know that. King Lear's daughters. We're studying that now." She handed him the Cliff Notes.

"Right. I never was too good with names, or literature." Grant laughed and thrust his hands into his pockets.

"You and me both." Cindy sighed. "But Mom is always trying to get me to read more. Nicole is a real whiz when it comes to that sort of stuff. Even Mollie reads more than I do—mostly magazines, though."

"But they can't surf the way you can." He put his hand into hers. "Want to go after classes today?"

Cindy shook her head. "Swim meet."

"I'll watch you."

"Oh, that's not necessary." She hadn't quite forgiven him for his behavior the other night, and the last thing she wanted to think about now was another dance.

"You know, I could swear it sounds as if you're angry with me. But I'm the one who should be angry with you. After all, you ruined my whole evening." He shook his head, and Cindy felt her temper rising.

"Excuse me." She pushed past him. "I have a class and I don't want to be late." She started down the hall and then turned. "Grant."

He stopped. From the look on his face, it was obvious that he expected her to apologize. But why should she apologize? All she'd done was care for a cat.

"What?" he finally said.

Cindy, aware that a few of Mollie's friends were listening in, decided not to say anything. "Nothing. I'll talk to you later." Cindy turned around and headed toward her next class.

Mollie came over to Cindy's table in study hall just as the period was about to start. The bell hadn't rung yet and she had a few moments to get to her own lit class. "Why'd you turn Grant down for Sadie Hawkins?"

Cindy stared at her sister. She couldn't believe it was all over school already!

"I didn't turn him down. I never answered him."

"You mean you're still going to go?"

"Nope. I mean for you to stay out of my business. You've got your own things to worry about, sister dear. Don't bother me about Grant. I don't want to hear about him."

"Well, he is right, you know. I mean, I could have taken Cinders to the vet."

Cindy merely glared at her sister.

"All right, so I couldn't have. But he could have driven me." Mollie paused. "But to change the subject, I have a favor to ask of you."

"What?"

Mollie handed her sister a dry-cleaning ticket. Sheepishly, she explained. "It's for Nicole's sweater. Stupid Brain English was at the movies and he was having a popcorn fight with Linda and Sarah."

"Oh, Mollie, no. Have you told Nicole? She's never even worn that sweater."

Mollie pursed her lips and shook her head. "No, I haven't told her. Maybe it will all come out." But Mollie looked doubtful. "How could I have known this would happen?"

"Nicole's going to kill you, if it doesn't."

"I know. I know. I just don't want her to see me at the cleaner's. She'd know for sure then. Besides, I'm supposed to be meeting Steve and his friends at Pete's later."

Cindy stared at the ticket and crammed it into her pocket. It really was out of her way. "Well, did it work? I mean, did Steve at least notice you?"

Mollie sighed and shook her head.

"But you're meeting him today at Pete's."

Mollie half turned away and tugged at her ponytail. "Well, actually, I overheard one of his friends say they were going there after school. So I figured—"

"Mollie ..."

But her sister had disappeared down the hall before Cindy could give her the lecture she so well deserved, or give her back the cleaner's ticket.

As she biked home from the swim meet, Cindy tried to push Grant out of her mind, but it wasn't easy. If she didn't think about Grant, then she thought about Nicole and the brides' magazines in Nicole's room. Surely, her sister couldn't be planning on doing anything so foolish as getting married.

Maybe this time she could get Nicole to talk to her. And now that Cindy had a better idea of what was going on, she'd ask the right questions. Mollie had failed, but that didn't mean she would. Or, at least, if Nicole was really going to run away and get married, she ought to tell her sisters. What good was a wedding without bridesmaids, bouquets, dancing, and all that stuff? And she knew that if she was upset at the idea of being left out of Nicole's wedding plans, Mollie would be heartbroken. Mollie had already planned her own wedding down to the smallest detail.

To Cindy's amazement, Nicole was home—studying.

"What's that?"

"Oh, nothing." Cindy put the package label-side-down on the buffet.

Nicole shrugged and put on the water for coffee and then turned off the flame, taking out a milk carton instead.

"Grant asked me to the Sadie Hawkins dance."

"He did?" Nicole smiled. "That's great. At least he's not upset with you for ruining his time at the dance."

"My ruining his time! You're as bad as he was. Nicole, Cinders was dying." As if knowing she was the topic of conversation, the cat wandered into the kitchen. Cindy picked her up and scratched her under the chin. The contented purr from the cat made Cindy smile.

"Cindy, sometimes you care too much about the animals and not enough about the people in your life."

"That's not true. But I think a stupid dance is far less important than a life."

Nicole smiled complacently and sipped her milk. "I'm not saying it is. But I think you're using the animals as a way of not letting Grant near you. Are you scared of him?"

"Me? Scared?" Cindy laughed, but she had to admit to herself that there was some truth behind Nicole's observation.

"Yes, you. Grant really likes you, Cindy. At least from what I can see. He's not going to eat you like the big bad wolf."

Cindy sighed. "Stop acting like Mom. It was bad enough when they were out of town. You don't have an excuse now, and you don't know everything."

"No, but I do have more experience with men than you."

Cindy shrugged. "So what if you do? Right now I'm more concerned about *you* than Grant. I think you ought to tell us what's up."

"What do you mean?" Nicole turned her back on Cindy and adjusted her French braid. "Nothing's up."

"Nicole. You can't keep on lying to us. If you're making any plans—"

"My plans don't concern you. You're getting to be as nosy as Mollie." She glanced at her watch. "I have an appointment." Nicole finished her milk, gathered up her books, and started out the door.

"An appointment? Who with?"

Nicole whirled around. "I'm a little tired of you two sneaking around and putting your nose in my business."

"But if you're in trouble . . ."

Her sister laughed. "Your imagination is worse than Mollie's! Don't worry, Cindy. Everything's fine. I'm not in any trouble. I promise. I'll tell you and Mollie everything when the time is right." With that, Nicole slammed the door.

But Cindy couldn't help but worry. Nicole usually didn't confide in Cindy, but she had never been this secretive before. In her smug, superior way, Nicole had always been honest, although tact had prevented her from blurting things out the way Cindy did.

Just then, Mollie flew into the kitchen, interrupting her thoughts.

"Where's Nicole?" Mollie asked glumly. Steve had never shown up at Pete's, so it had been a wasted afternoon.

"Just left," Cindy grunted.

"Well?"

"Well what?"

"What did you learn?"

"Not much," Cindy informed her sister, "except I think she's in love with this Alain guy and we'd better tell Mom and Dad before she does something stupid, like getting married."

"Gosh, no! We can't say anything. Mother and Dad would kill her if they knew. You really think she might be getting married?" Mollie had a slight smile on her face. "At least Alain is awfully handsome."

"And awfully old," Cindy added. "I hope we're doing the right thing. I'm beginning to think we should tell Mom. Nicole could ruin her whole life."

"But it's so romantic."

"Grow up, Mollie. It's not romantic; it's ridiculous." Cindy almost shouted at her sister, fed up with Mollie's childish behavior. She paused to calm herself. "I don't want to talk about this until we have more proof of what Nicole is up to." She motioned to the package.

"There's the sweater I picked up for you. You're lucky. She almost saw me."

Mollie looked contrite. "You're a great sister." She leaned over and kissed Cindy impulsively. "What would I do without you?" She grabbed a peanut butter cookie from the jar. "What are we going to do about Nicole?"

"I'm getting tired of that question. Somehow we have to show her that she'd be making a big mistake."

Mollie nodded and took another cookie.

"They allowed on your diet?"

"Yeah, peanut butter is protein." Mollie put her feet up on the table. "I still think it's romantic. Imagine. Nicole running off to get married." Mollie closed her eyes and hummed the wedding march, while Cindy threw a pot holder at her sister and left the kitchen to think things over rationally.

Chapter 11

$\mathcal{M}$ollie slammed her math book closed in disgust. "This is really stupid." She took a bite of her taco and glanced up at Sarah.

The three girls were once again gathered at their favorite hangout. Mollie hoped that she could summon up the courage to ask Steve to the Sadie Hawkins. He was sitting a few tables away with several freshman guys. But not once had he looked in her direction.

"The reason this sounds so stupid," Sarah the brain said, "is because you're not reading properly. You're hoping that Master Steve will walk over."

Mollie shrugged. She wasn't going to deny it. "So? He can help me with math."

Linda laughed and took a sip of Mollie's Coke. "You're a worse schemer than my sister. I don't know how Liz gets any work done. She's always thinking about the cute boys and dates and dances."

"Well, you do, too."

Linda shook her head. "Not as much as she does—or you, for that matter." She paused. "Though I wouldn't mind if Brian would pay some attention to me. He's really nice!" She protested as both Mollie and Sarah made faces.

"Revenge of the nerds, part three!" Mollie whispered. "Hey, look, here he comes now. And—" Mollie's words stopped in mid-sentence. Grant was with him. Now, why would Grant be walking in with the queerest boy at Vista?

Grant, seeing Mollie, excused himself and headed toward her table. His hand touched her shoulder. "Mollie, hi!"

She looked up, as if startled. "Oh, hi, Grant." It wouldn't hurt to be seen talking with Grant. With any luck, Steve didn't know he was Mollie's sister's boyfriend.

"Mollie, I need to talk to you a moment."

"You do?"

"Yeah, it's about your sister. I want to know what's with her. She's ..."

Mollie sucked in her breath. Steve was looking over at them.

"Sit down!" She pulled Grant into the chair

beside her. "I'd love to talk to you." Mollie gave Grant all her attention, pretending to ignore Steve, though she couldn't help watching him out of the corner of her eye. "Ask me anything you want."

Sarah couldn't suppress a giggle.

Grant's brow furrowed. Why was Mollie acting so silly? He didn't understand until he looked back at Steve's table. "Oh, I see." He shrugged. "You Lewis sisters love to play games, don't you? Well, I don't think I want to be any part of your latest game." He stood.

"Grant, wait." Mollie pulled at his sleeve. "I thought you wanted to ask me something about Cindy?"

He looked at her hand on his arm and then at her. "I did, but forget it." Freeing himself, he turned and walked away.

"You blew it, kid," Linda stated. "Not only for yourself, but for Cindy. I bet he's going over to Steve right now to tell him all about you."

"He wouldn't."

"He would and he is," Sarah pointed out as the girls watched Grant go over and sit down at Steve's table. Steve was a freshman, like they were, and Grant was a junior. There was absolutely no reason for Grant to be sitting with Steve—unless he was tattling on her. Mollie's heart sank.

"Well, Cindy was right about him. He's heartless. She can get better than that." Mollie took a deep breath and tried to turn her attention back to the math. After all, that was why they were studying together. Those tests Mr. Alexander gave weren't easy.

"You think I should ask Steve to come over and explain this equation for us?"

"I dare you." Linda grinned.

Mollie met her eyes. "Them there's fightin' words, ma'am." Mollie stood.

"You're actually going to?" Sarah was aghast.

"A Lewis never backs down from a dare. Must be from our Scottish great-great-grandparents." She picked up her math book. "Be back in a flash with the cash—or at least the answer." She gave the other two a smile and wondered if they really knew how nervous she was. Her knees were shaking and her mouth felt dry.

As she started to approach, she realized that she just couldn't do it. Stopping a few feet short of the table, she overheard one of the guys asking Steve, "You mean you're going with Barbara C.?"

She felt as if someone had socked her in the stomach. Her knees were like water now. If one of Cindy's giant waves had come by, she would have been rolled over and drowned.

Horrified, she knew she couldn't possibly ask him for help with her math. She'd find someone else to help her. Someone who would appreciate her.

Mollie took a step backward and backed into

something. She felt something wet drip down her back as she tumbled to the ground.

A tray of tacos, nachos, cheese dip, sour cream, and soda rained over her and the waitress.

"Oh, yuck," Mollie screeched, trying to wipe some of the stuff off her blouse. Steve turned to see what the commotion was and burst out laughing as he saw the cheese and sour cream dripping from Mollie's hair.

She glared at him, furious. It was his fault. If he hadn't been talking to his friends about Barbara C., if he had paid any attention to her at all, this never would have happened.

Looking around, Mollie noticed that the entire restaurant was laughing at her. Even Linda and Sarah.

Without speaking, Mollie picked up her salsa-sauce-stained math book and ran into the washroom.

Linda and Sarah, still laughing, followed her.

"You have to admit you do look a sight." Sarah tried to keep a straight face.

Mollie frowned at her reflection in the mirror. Maybe she did, but that wasn't why Steve had passed her up to go to the dance with Barbara C. Maybe ... maybe it was because she was so ugly. In the sink, she tried to wash the sour cream from her hair, but it didn't do any good.

Tears veiled her vision. It wasn't fair. Mollie stared again at her mirror image. No wonder Steve didn't like her. She was fatter than Barbara C. Mostly because she'd spent so much time lately at Taco Rio. "Darn!" She tried again to get some of the cheese out of her jeans. Well, she'd let Mom clean them up.

"Why didn't you go up to him like you said you would? If you hadn't backed away so suddenly, this never would have happened."

Mollie glared at Linda. "That oaf is going with Barbara C. How could he? How could he?" Mollie wailed as she started to pull at her hair. A clump of cheese came off in her hands. "Look at this! Now I've made a fool of myself in front of everybody—including Grant and ... Rafael Martin."

"He was here?"

"Didn't you see? He was in the corner of the room." Tears sparkled in Mollie's blue eyes. "He was laughing just like everyone else. Oh, what am I going to do? Now I'll never go to the Sadie Hawkins dance. I'll never go to any dance at all. My life is ruined. I might as well go off and join the French Foreign Legion—or something. But I'm only barely passing in French." She giggled, recovering a bit of her sense of humor.

"We'll get you out of here, Mollie. You can go home and clean up."

"I'm not leaving this bathroom looking like this," Mollie screeched.

"That's okay. Linda's already called your house.

Nicole's coming over with some clean clothes for you."

"Nicole is?" Mollie squeaked. She was surprised that Nicole was even home now. "When did she say she'd be here?"

"Five minutes, max. She's driving over."

"Listen, do me a favor," Mollie pleaded as she looked into her mirror image—the witch the sea dredged up! "Don't say anything about what I told you."

"You mean about the wedding?" Sarah asked.

"Wedding?" The bathroom door opened and revealed Nicole standing in the archway, holding a bag of clothes for Mollie. "Who's getting married? Not one of you, I hope."

"No! Oh, no." Mollie recovered quickly. "Sarah was talking about our, um, home ec assignment. You know, Mr. Peterson wants us all to pair up and pretend to be married."

"Oh?" Nicole lifted a brow. "Hmm. I'll have to talk to him. That might make an interesting feature for the yearbook. Who did you pair up with?"

"Oh, no. You can't talk to him. Not yet. I mean, he just mentioned today that we were going to be doing it later in the semester. We haven't picked partners yet. So, wait. Okay?" Mollie glanced at her two friends for support. "I'll let you know as soon as we have something."

"Yeah," Linda added. "He wasn't even sure we'd have time this semester."

Nicole looked at Mollie and Linda and then shrugged. "Whatever. Anyway, Mol, here's some fresh clothes so we can get you home. Then you and I can talk."

Mollie nodded and quickly changed.

Back home, after she had showered and washed her hair, Mollie flopped down on Nicole's bed. It was just like it used to be—before Nicole became a spy, or decided to run away and get married, or whatever it was she was doing.

"I was so mortified, Nicole. I mean, I was the laughing stock."

"Oh, Mollie, accidents happen."

"Yeah?" Mollie found herself studying Nicole and wondering if accidents had ever happened to her sister. She doubted it. Nicole was always so poised, so confident of herself and her ability.

"Yes." Nicole ruffled Mollie's now dry hair. "Even to me. Once, when I was a freshman, I got caught in the middle of the lawn when all of a sudden all the sprinklers turned on. I was completely soaked." Nicole laughed. "And Mrs. Steinhauser made me change and put on my gym clothes and wear a lab smock over it! I was mortified. I had to go to classes all morning dressed like that."

Mollie giggled. "You never told me about that."

"I didn't tell *anyone*, Mollie. I thought I would die of embarrassment."

"Still"—Mollie sobered up—"that wasn't your

fault. This was all my own doing—all because of Steve."

"He isn't worth it, Mol."

"But Steve was so ... nice to me before. I was sure he wanted to take me out. Then suddenly he turned into an A-One jerk. I mean, he went to the Alta California dance alone.... He knew how much I wanted to go ... and then he ... he lets Barbara take him to the Sadie Hawkins dance."

Nicole shrugged. "If he agreed to go with Barbara, then maybe he wasn't right for you." She patted Mollie's shoulder. "You'll find someone else. I promise." She thought for a moment. "Hey, you know, we just had a new sophomore, a transfer student from Los Angeles, join the yearbook. His name is ..." She paused. "Raymond Hamilton."

Mollie frowned. "I don't need my big sister to fix me up. Besides, you have enough problems of your own."

"Mol, I won't fix you up. I promise. Just come by one of the meetings after school and you'll meet him yourself."

Mollie sat upright on the bed. "You're going to the meetings now? Cindy said that Bitsy said—"

"When are you going to learn to stop repeating gossip?"

"Well, it's just that I heard you weren't going to any of your meetings. I mean, you have been acting kind of strange lately."

Nicole rolled her eyes. "Preoccupied might be a better word."

"About?"

"About ..." Nicole glanced at her watch. "Oh, gosh, it's nearly time for Mom to come home. I'd better go set the table."

"I'll help," Mollie said, following her sister out of the room—but not before she had another quick look around.

Chapter 12

"*B*ut what did she say?" Cindy shouted above the noise of a new album that Mollie and her friends were playing.

"I told you, Cin. All she would say is that she was preoccupied about something, and she told me to forget about Steve. She wants to introduce me to someone named Raymond on the yearbook."

"That means she's going to her meetings again, so maybe everything's all right," Linda put in.

"I sure hope so. But I have the feeling it's not." Cindy turned down the stereo.

"Why?" Mollie wanted to know.

Cindy sighed. "Because she had another phone call tonight and ran out just after you guys came upstairs. I think whatever was going on is still going on."

"You should have followed her."

"With what? Mental vision?" Cindy gave her younger sister a light punch in the arm. "My dear sister, Nicole has the car keys. And even if I did know where to go, my bike has a flat."

"Then we have to trick her into telling us the whole story." Mollie stamped her foot. "It's about time we learned. After all"—she stuck her lower lip out—"we are her sisters. We're supposed to help one another."

"Yeah." Cindy glanced at the two girls and then again at her sister. "Like you helped me this afternoon with Grant."

"Aw, Cindy, that's not fair. How was I to know Grant would figure it out? I had to do something." Mollie pleaded for her sister's forgiveness. "The situation was desperate. Really, it was."

Cindy sighed. "Well, it doesn't matter anyway. I heard that Susan Sedaris is going with him to Sadie Hawkins. So ..." She shrugged and picked up Winston's front paws. "Care to dance, big boy?"

Winston woofed his agreement and jumped about while Mollie sighed over her latest blunder. Had she really ruined things for Cindy and Grant?

Bitsy paced the hall in front of the gym as she waited for Cindy to come out.

"It's about time. Are you always so tardy for important meetings?"

Cindy bent down to relace her sneakers. "I had to finish tallying the scores. Besides, this isn't all that important, Bitsy."

"Says you. You don't know what a total crisis I'm going through. My best friend might be running away, and it's not important? Some loyal sister you are. So, am I going to be a bridesmaid?"

It was tiresome dealing with people like Bitsy and Mollie, who made such mountains out of molehills. "We don't know anything yet. We only know that we found some brides' magazines in her room. That doesn't mean anything, really." Cindy sighed, trying to convince herself. "And I still think you should ask her outright. She might be worried we'd tell Mom or Dad. But you she'd probably tell."

"I don't think so, and I'm getting a little tired of trying to drag everything out of her." Bitsy tossed her head, sending her short blonde curls swaying. "Maybe she's the one who should be worried. At this rate, she won't have any friends left." Bitsy picked up her books and hurried down the hall.

Cindy stared after Bitsy for a few minutes and then continued on her way. If Nicole really was having the problems that Mollie and Bitsy imagined, then Cindy was sure that her sister would have confided in them by now. Wouldn't she?

Each time Cindy had tried to talk to Nicole,

something had interrupted the conversation—a phone call, or Nicole running out to a "meeting," or just plain being turned off. But Cindy was sure that her sister, with all of her brains, was too smart to allow her whole life to be ruined by an early marriage.

Surely, Nicole could see that if she married now, she'd never get to Paris for her junior year abroad, which she was always talking about. Maybe it was time to talk to Mom and let her deal with Nicole, but then if Nicole was hiding something really big, she'd probably never forgive Cindy.

Cindy sighed. It was hard enough dealing with her own problems with Grant and with Mollie's heartache over Steve's rejection. Why couldn't everything be nice for a change?

She was suddenly aware of someone walking beside her. Looking up, she realized that it was Grant.

"Hi, Cindy."

"Hi." She kept on walking, not wanting him to notice how pleased she was to see him.

"Hey. Wait up." He put his arm on hers.

"Why? So you can tell me you're taking Susan Sedaris to the Sadie Hawkins dance? How long did it take for her to step in after the school gossips told her I wasn't going with you?"

"Cindy, that's what I wanted to talk to you about. I just heard about my supposed date with Susan."

She stopped where she was, despite the fact that the second bell was ringing, and all around her, everyone was running to class. "What do you mean, you just heard? Didn't she ask you? Didn't you accept? From what I heard, you practically jumped at her invitation and you're planning to have dinner at her parents' country club before the party."

Grant gave a sheepish grin. "Oh, she asked me, all right, and yeah, she said we could go to the dinner at the club. But I told her no." He touched her hand briefly. "I was hoping that we'd go."

Cindy didn't move his hand. She didn't want to. All she could think of was Grant, of the warmth of his hand, and of what he had just said. He was giving her another chance.

The final bell rang. "I have English lit."

"So do I. But Cindy ..." He paused and looked down the nearly empty hall. "I wanted to tell you that I was wrong in what I said. About your cats, I mean. I can understand how Cinders's being hurt would mean so much to you. After all, you raised her from a kitten."

Cindy's mouth dropped open. "How did you know?"

"Mollie." He grinned. "That sister of yours is a good source of information."

Cindy narrowed her eyes.

"Don't be angry with her. Please. I asked her. I wanted to understand, and I want us to be a team again. No one plays tennis like you, and certainly no one surfs like you. Being with the others is no contest at all."

"You want to be with me just because I'm a contest?" Cindy started to walk on.

He wouldn't let go of her. "No, silly. I want to be with you because I want to be with you. I like you."

"Oh."

There was a pause. Mrs. Milson, the vice-principal, walked by. "You young people had better hurry. I don't want to give you any demerits."

"Yes, ma'am." Grant nodded to her.

To Cindy he said, "So, do you ask me to Sadie Hawkins, or do I have to change my name again?"

Mrs. Milson was glaring at them.

Cindy paused, but only slightly. "Will you go with me to Sadie Hawkins?"

"Sure. Anytime."

Cindy's face brightened. "I gotta run. Talk to you later."

"See you at Pete's. My treat." He leaned over and kissed her quickly on the lips—in front of the disapproving Mrs. Milson. Cindy flushed and ran down the hall.

The rest of the day flew by. Even seeing Mollie and her gang gathered at the pizza place rather than Taco Rio didn't bother her.

Cindy did wonder where Nicole was, though.

She hadn't seen her older sister at all today; usually, they bumped into each other at least once in the hall. But then she had been so preoccupied with seeing Grant later that Nicole might have passed by her ten times in the hall and Cindy wouldn't have noticed.

It was nearly time for dinner when Cindy walked into the house. Mollie had arrived home just a few minutes earlier. Mrs. Lewis was still in the kitchen, getting things ready for dinner. Cindy could tell they were having something new tonight, because Mom always closed the kitchen door when she was trying out a new recipe.

"Tell Nicole to get ready," Mrs. Lewis said as Cindy walked in. "We'll be eating in fifteen minutes."

"Sure," Cindy replied, pouring food into Winston's bowl and giving each of the cats a treat. She smiled to herself as she started out of the kitchen and up the stairs. Everything was turning out just fine. She was sure that Nicole's mystery would soon clear up, too. But on the stairway, she was met by a horrified Mollie.

"What's wrong? What did Steve do this time?"

Mollie merely shook her head.

"Well, what's wrong?"

Mollie continued to stare at her as if the whole world had collapsed. Cindy had never seen her sister like this. If anything, she usually jabbered away in a crisis.

"Mollie, what happened?" Cindy insisted again.

Shaking her head, her blue eyes looking as if she had just seen a ghost, Mollie handed Cindy a note written on Nicole's pink and white stationery.

"Read it." Mollie's voice was hoarse.

Puzzled, Cindy took the note.

Dear Cindy and Mollie:

Please don't let this letter upset you. I've gone to Los Angeles overnight. Tell Mom I'm with Bitsy. I promise I'll explain everything when I get back. Mom wasn't around, so I couldn't tell her.

Love, Nicole

Cindy turned the note around. "Nothing else? This is all?"

Mollie nodded. "What are we going to tell Mom?"

"You're right. This is terrible." Cindy dragged her younger sister up to Nicole's room. "We're going to search this place, find out where she is, and go after her. I hate to admit it, Mollie, but I think you're right. Nicole really must be in some trouble."

The two girls began searching through the drawers in their sister's room.

"The bridal magazines are gone."

"Yeah, and so is her blue sweater," Mollie added.

"I wonder if she noticed the stain still on it." She made a face.

Cindy glanced around again, ignoring her sister. They had looked everywhere and hadn't found anything that could help them.

"The desk. We haven't looked in her desk."

Cindy went over to the white French table and pulled at the drawer. It was locked.

"Wait a minute." Mollie ran to get a bobby pin from their mother's bathroom. She returned a moment later and, using the bobby pin, began fiddling with the lock on the drawer. "I saw it done on *Remington Steele*."

"Mollie, it's not—"

Before Cindy could finish her sentence, they both heard a click, and the drawer slid open. Mollie had an "I told you so" expression on her face.

There didn't seem to be any clues in the drawer, however. Mollie pulled it open further.

Nothing. Idly, Cindy picked up some of the papers in the drawer. Because Nicole was so neat, it seemed odd to find them lying any old way.

"Look at this!" she told her sister. "Addresses."

"So?"

"Mollie, you're the one with the imagination. I bet these are places Nicole went to in L.A."

Mollie grabbed the paper from Cindy, and her eyes widened. "Yeah."

Suddenly Cindy felt a strangeness in the pit of

her stomach. She shook her head, unwilling to believe what she was thinking, and she sank down onto the bed. "Mollie, how could we have been so blind? You're right. Nicole's run off, but not because she's a spy. She's in love, and she's run off to get married."

"Oh, no, she can't do that! She'll ruin her life. She ..." Mollie turned to Cindy. "You didn't believe me before. Why do you believe me now?"

"Because," Cindy explained, "I was talking with Nicole the other morning, and she got all glowy and talked about love. But why would she run away now? Couldn't she have at least waited until summer?"

Mollie sank down on the bed beside her sister. "Cin, we've got to stop her before she makes a mistake."

"Yeah, how? We gonna fly to L.A.? Or maybe ride our bikes?"

Mollie shook her head. There were tears in her eyes now. "We have to think of something. We can't let Nicole do this, at least not without our being there. Someone has to drive us."

Cindy sighed. "The only one I know who has a license is Bitsy, and she's ..."

Cinders came into the room just then and jumped on the bed. Curled up next to the stuffed monkey, it reminded Mollie of Grant.

"What about Grant? He has a car."

Cindy pressed her lips together tightly. She really didn't want to ask him, but Mollie was right.

Other than Bitsy, who would be a nervous wreck, Grant was the only one.

"You have to call him, Cin. He can drive us to L.A. and check out these addresses. She might be in a lot of trouble."

Cindy stared at her sister for a moment and then stood. "All right. I'll call him."

"Well, what are we waiting for?"

"You're staying here and talking to Mom."

"I am not."

"Mollie, someone has to do it."

"Nicole's my sister, too. I'm just as worried about her as you are. I'm going."

"And Grant's *my* boyfriend."

Mollie opened her mouth. "You're going with him to the dance, then." Her eyes sparkled. "Great. I knew it would work."

"What would work?" Cindy felt her stomach tighten.

Mollie merely shrugged and started to turn away.

Cindy grabbed her sister's shoulders as if to throttle her. "Mollie ..."

Mollie looked down and mumbled, "I just played on his sympathy and told him how lonely you were without him and how much you adored him, how you had a picture of him, and how you slept with it under your pillow...."

With each word, Cindy felt herself slowly dying. No wonder Grant had been so sweet to her today.

"I also told him how you had raised Cinders

from a kitten and that's why she meant so much to you."

There was murder in Cindy's eyes, but she couldn't do anything about it now.

"Cindy, please let me go with you to Los Angeles. Besides, there are several addresses here. We might need to check out more than one place, especially if we're going to reach her in time."

Her lips pressed together, Cindy nodded slightly. Two heads were better than one, although Cindy doubted that Mollie could be counted on to keep her head. Still, Cindy knew that Mollie was in some ways closer to Nicole than she was, and it was only right that her younger sister come along.

"All right. But if you say one word to Grant about *anything,* Mollie Lewis, so help me I'll—"

"Girls! Dinner's ready!" Mrs. Lewis's voice floated up.

Mollie looked at Cindy and then at the note. "What are we going to tell Mom?"

"You're the one with the imagination. You figure it out."

Chapter 13

"*What do you mean, Nicole is spending the night at Bitsy's?*" Mrs. Lewis asked as everyone sat down to dinner. "Why did she go there? And more important, why didn't she tell me?"

"I don't know, Mom. She had this phone call when I was upstairs," Mollie lied, "and she said that her friend Marcella—you know, the French girl—was going to be calling at Bitsy's so they could both talk. You know how Nicole is when she gets on the phone," Mollie improvised. "No one can use it for hours."

"Sounds like someone else I know." Mrs. Lewis smiled at her youngest. "Well, I guess that's okay. But you girls should ask first, before you go running off."

Both girls looked at each other and nodded.

While their dad told their mother about his latest project, Cindy and Mollie attacked the food.

Mr. Lewis paused as Cindy, having gobbled her dinner in record speed, pushed away from the table. "What's the hurry, Cindy?"

"Uh"—she looked at Mollie—"I have this history paper. I'm going over to Anna's to work on it."

Mr. Lewis nodded. "And you, Mollie?"

"Going to Linda's. Got to study for math."

Under the table, Mollie kicked Cindy before she could say anything to hurt the cause.

Cindy stood and kissed her mother and father good-bye, nearly colliding with Mollie, who stood at the same time. "Watch it, klutz!"

Mollie glared at her sister.

"You leaving, too?"

"Yeah, Mom. I am."

"All right. Both of you be home by ten-thirty."

"Sure, Mom. We know." Cindy grabbed her jacket. Winston jumped up, thinking that he was being taken for a walk. "No, boy. Not now. Later." She pushed the dog away and watched him go to a corner and sulk.

"Thought you'd try to leave me behind, did you?" Mollie hissed as they both walked out the door.

"Mol, I just don't want—"

"Look, I give you my solemn Girl Scout word. I

won't say anything to Grant." She lifted her leg over the bike as Cindy did the same.

"All right. Follow me."

"Oh, I already know the way to Grant's."

Cindy stared as her sister started off. Sometimes Mollie, she thought, sometimes . . .

At Grant's house, Cindy paced up and down the living room as she tried to tell him the story. It wasn't easy—especially as he kept frowning. She could tell he didn't believe a word she was saying. But then who would? She hadn't believed Mollie either.

"Listen, all we want is for you to drive us to Los Angeles."

"To check out addresses of places you don't even know about." Grant looked from one girl to the other. "Okay. Let's go."

"You'll take us?" Cindy looked relieved.

"Of course," Grant nodded, holding the front door open for Mollie and Cindy.

"I hope we're doing the right thing," Cindy said to Mollie as they sat in the car.

"We are. How else can we find Nicole and stop her?"

Cindy nodded. All she could think of were those bridal magazines and the expression on her sister's face when she had talked about love.

They drove along the winding, dark road that led to Highway 101 and Los Angeles.

*   *   *

The drive down to Los Angeles was awkward at first, as Grant asked more questions about Nicole's activities. At first Mollie refused to talk to Grant at all, until Cindy realized what she was doing and glared at her. Given the go-ahead, Mollie answered—with all of her wild ideas.

Finally, Grant burst out laughing. "Mollie, have you ever thought of being a writer? You have a terrific imagination.

"Yeah, don't I?" Mollie smiled and looked out the window.

Melrose Avenue in Los Angeles, the first address, was like a totally different universe from quiet Santa Barbara. The street was filled with punk rockers with purple hair and green nail polish and outfits that shouted color. They were wilder than even Mollie could imagine.

"Oh, my." She stared at them, then at her own outfit—jeans and a fuzzy pink sweater.

"This way." Grant directed her to the top of a two-story building.

The first room they went to was opened by a tall, bald guy dressed in black leather and chains. Music blared from inside. Even Cindy was amazed. Through the open door, she was able to peek into the red velvet room.

"Yeah? What d'ya want?" The guard studied the trio.

"Uh, we're looking for someone," Cindy piped up.

"Who?"

"Nicole. Nicole Lewis."

"She ain't here."

"You mean, she was?" Mollie couldn't believe her sister would actually come to a place like this.

The guard shrugged, slamming the door before either of the girls could ask anything more.

Cindy could only stare at the closed door, while Grant urged them to leave.

Walking down the stairs, Mollie said, "Maybe Nicole's a secret punker."

"If any of the Lewises were a secret punker, Mollie, it would be you," Grant laughed. "Or maybe even Cindy, but definitely not Nicole. Let's go."

The next address was also on Melrose, but farther down, at a place called "The Wedding Chapel." Neon lights flashed "24-Hour Service."

Cindy stood outside the door and looked up at the sign. "I don't know if I even want to go in."

"I think I feel faint," Mollie said, echoing her sister's words.

"Maybe we're not too late," Grant tried to console the girls as he opened the door.

The jingling of the bell above sounded like Santa Claus's sleigh, but this place certainly wasn't his toy workshop.

"Can I help you?" A short, balding man came out to talk to Grant. Then he looked at the two girls. "My, my, and so young." He peered through his specs. "Just how old are you, son?"

Before Grant could answer and explain that he had no intention of getting married to Mollie or to Cindy, the man continued.

"You know there are rules which"—he sighed—"alas, I must abide by. I can't marry people underage. I—"

Mollie interrupted, "How under is underage?"

He studied her briefly. "Technically? Eighteen. I can fudge things by a few months, perhaps." He grinned. "But I think you need to wait a bit."

Mollie glanced at her sister. "Do you think—"

"Have you married anyone tonight?" Cindy interrupted, digging her elbow into Mollie's ribs.

"Tonight?" The man shrugged. "I'd have to check my records."

"He wants a bribe," Mollie whispered a little too loudly to Cindy.

"How do you know?"

"Trust me," Mollie said.

"We don't want to get married ourselves," Cindy explained as Mollie smiled. "We're looking for our sister. Nicole Lewis. Has she been in here?"

"Lots of people been in here. Can't say I know the name."

Grant took a ten-dollar bill from his wallet as

he glanced at Mollie. "Sir, it would help us to know if Nicole was here."

Greedily, the little man snapped up the money. "How old is she, and what's she look like?"

"Like an older version of me," Mollie said. "Only prettier."

"And taller," Cindy added.

He stared at her a moment more. "Yep. She was here, I think. Only she didn't stay long."

"She was!" Cindy, Mollie, and Grant said in unison.

"What? Girl with light brown hair and blue eyes came in 'round 'bout six. Had three men with her. Mind, one seemed rather special."

"Did you marry her to any of them?"

"Nope. Can't say as I did. No proof of her age, as I recall. They paid me to use the chapel for a bit, so I let them be. Then they left. Real pretty gown she wore, too. Nicest wedding dress I seen here in a long time."

Mollie gasped.

"Do you know where they might have gone?" Grant asked, taking charge.

"Nope. Can't say as I do, but if I see them again, I'll let them know you're looking."

"Right. Thanks." Grant took Cindy on one arm and Mollie on the other, ushering both girls out.

Cindy was stunned as she looked back. "Mollie, could he really have been talking about Nicole?"

"Why don't we check that last address?" Grant said.

"I'm afraid it's hopeless."

"No, Cindy," Mollie put her hand on her older sister. "Don't say that yet. After all, the guy in there said he hadn't married them. Which means this next place we're going to ... I mean, we might still be in time."

Cindy closed her eyes. "I hope so."

The last address was located in the posh Los Angeles area of Brentwood.

The house was even grander than the one to which Mollie had followed Nicole.

"Are you sure this is right? I mean, it's nothing like the other two places," Cindy asked, taking the paper from her sister.

"Certainly seems so." Grant looked over her shoulder and checked. "Shall we go in?"

Cindy looked at the mansion and then back at her sister and then to Grant. "I guess we might as well."

It took several minutes before someone answered the door.

"Can I help you?" asked a man dressed like a butler.

"Uh, yeah." Mollie tried to peer in at his side. "We're looking for—"

Suddenly Mollie saw Nicole in the formal living room. She was standing near the fireplace, dressed in a flowing satin white bridal gown, next to a handsome man in a tux. The same man she had seen in Montecito!

"No, Nicole, Stop! You can't do this! You're making a dreadful mistake. You—" Mollie rushed past the butler before he could stop her, and Cindy quickly followed.

"What the—" The man at Nicole's side turned. "Nicole, who are these girls? What are they blabbering about?"

Nicole turned a shade of pink, then red. "Yes, what are you two doing here?" She looked furious.

"Oh, Nicole, Nicole, don't you realize what a mistake you're making? Are we too late?" Mollie tugged at her sister's hand and looked up at Nicole's now bewildered expression.

"What are you talking about, Mollie?"

"This." Mollie touched the wedding dress and turned around, suddenly realizing that they weren't alone with Nicole, her husband-to-be, and the judge. There was a whole roomful of people, all dressed in flannel shirts and jeans. They certainly didn't look like wedding guests!

It was Mollie's and Cindy's turn to be bewildered.

"Alain, can we take a few minutes' break? I need to talk to these two."

"Sure." The man next to Nicole nodded and, gracefully picking up her train so that it wouldn't get dirty, Nicole led her two sisters into an alcove where a huge coffee pot had been set up.

"Nicole, what *is* happening?" Cindy finally asked.

"Yeah, where are the CIA men and the Russians? Why did you get married without us?" Mollie wanted to know.

"Mol!" Cindy tried to stop her.

Nicole started to laugh. "What?" She wiped away her tears and then sighed. "This certainly has gotten out of hand. I guess I should have told you guys sooner, but as you can see, I didn't run away to get married." She shook her head. "You, especially, should have known me better than that, Mol."

"But Nicole," Cindy said, "The way you were talking the other day ... I mean, about love and all that, and then Mollie followed you to this guy's house, and we found those brides' magazines in your room, and ..."

"And just what were you guys doing in my room and following me around?"

"We were worried about you!" Mollie practically screamed. "I think it's about time you tell us everything. Now!" Mollie glared back at her oldest sister. "What about telling me you wanted to visit Russia? What was that about?" Mollie waved her finger at her sister.

"Mollie," Nicole sighed again. "I never said I wanted to visit Russia. *You* asked me if I'd ever like to go there, and I said maybe."

"Oh, yeah, right." Mollie glanced at her feet. "But I still want to know what's happening."

"I really should be furious with you both. It's a good thing that Alain is so understanding."

"You're evading us," Cindy said.

Nicole waved her hand toward the living room. "I would think it would be obvious. We were taking photos."

"Photos?"

"For *Bride's* magazine. I'm modeling."

Both Cindy and Mollie's mouths dropped again. "But—"

"I didn't want to tell you or Mom and Dad before because I was afraid they would forbid it and say I couldn't handle it all. I wasn't sure I'd be able to do it, either, so I guess I didn't want anyone to know, in case I failed. Everyone always thinks I can do anything, but I wasn't so sure," Nicole admitted.

"But you couldn't handle it—not the modeling, I mean. Nicole, I saw those failed tests."

"And you never went to any of your club meetings, and Bitsy was complaining about missing you all the time."

"Yes," Nicole admitted, "I suppose you're right. At the beginning, I was trying to do too much and I didn't schedule my time very well. I mean, it wasn't easy getting my portfolio together and doing my schoolwork and keeping up with you all. But I have it under control now. And I plan on modeling only during the summer." She glanced at Mollie and patted her hand. "Really, I do. And I suppose all this is partly my fault. I knew you guys were curious and at one point I was going to tell you. But everybody was being so sneaky. Trying to trick me. I suppose I was annoyed that everyone was prying into my life, so I got stubborn. You should understand that, Cindy." Cindy nodded.

Nicole's arms went about both her sisters. "I love you guys—even if you are interfering sneaks."

"I guess we'd better call Mom and Dad and tell her that we're all in Los Angeles. We can stay at Aunt Kate's.

"All four of us?"

"Four?" Nicole looked up. She saw Grant for the first time as he came over and put his arm around Cindy.

"How else did you think we got down here? Mom'd never let me drive the car. I don't have a license."

"Well, the more the merrier, I guess." Nicole stood. "I have to finish these pictures now. I'll call and explain everything and tell Mom and Dad where we are."

"You'd better. Or we'll be in trouble."

As she headed back toward the living room,

Nicole smiled at her sisters. "I don't know about you, Cindy, but Mollie's already in trouble."

"Me?" Mollie squeaked.

"*Oui*, you owe me a blue angora sweater."

Chapter 14

As they rode back to Santa Barbara the following morning, Cindy found herself thinking about Grant. She realized that if everyone at school and at home had minded their own business and not made such a big deal over everything she and Grant did, she would probably have felt a lot more comfortable with him. And a dance couldn't be all that bad.

"I still don't understand why you didn't tell us anything," Mollie said, pouting.

"Because," Nicole repeated for the umpteenth time, "I wanted it to be a surprise—a *fait accompli.* I wanted to have my first assignment and—"

"But you did," Mollie interrupted.

"*Oui.* Last night." She looked at Mollie. "You

144

stop asking questions and I won't ask about my blue sweater."

"Oh." Mollie lowered her eyes. "All right," she sighed. "Still, I think it would have been interesting if Alain had been a Russian."

Cindy met Grant's eyes. "As I said before, Mollie Lewis," he laughed, "you really ought to consider becoming a writer."

"Back home, Nicole proudly showed her parents her portfolio. She had explained everything to them the night before, and after the initial shock had worn off, they didn't seem very upset.

"But darling, you can't be a model now. What about college? What about ..." During the night, Mrs. Lewis had become worried about Nicole's plans.

"Oh, Mom." Nicole kissed Mrs. Lewis. "I have no intention of dropping my plans for college. This is just a way for me to make some extra money during the summer."

"Hmm." Mr. Lewis put his glasses on and studied the photos. "That would be nice. You look beautiful, Nicole. But it won't interfere with your classes now, will it?"

Nicole glanced at Mollie.

Mollie knew she was thinking of those few tests she'd failed. Nicole had already explained that it was because she had gone off to the modeling class and hadn't studied. She had been trying to do too much at once—but she knew how to balance things now.

"Of course not. Believe me, Dad; I have everything under control."

Mr. Lewis gave her a hug. "That's my girl. You always do."

Up in her room with her friends the following day, Cindy thought that her older sister might have things under control, but she herself didn't.

"You don't want that." Anna pulled the plate of brownies away from Cindy as music played in the background. "You'll never fit into your dress."

Cindy frowned.

"Don't tell us you're having second thoughts about this dance, too," Carey said.

"No . . ." Cindy reached for the plate. "I guess I'm nervous. I mean, I . . ."

"But Cin, it'll be a breeze," Mollie said from the doorway.

"What are you doing listening in?"

Mollie grinned. "Grant's on the phone."

"Oh." Cindy stood. "I'll be right back. Don't eat any more of those cookies," she warned the others, "especially you, Mollie."

She returned to the room a few minutes later. "He wanted to know if we could double with Sam and Andrea."

Carey was aghast. Sam was the school president and, next to Rafael Martin, one of the handsomest guys around. Being seen with Grant and Sam wouldn't hurt Cindy any. "I hope you said yes."

Cindy nodded. "I said I didn't see anything wrong with it. We could do whatever he wanted."

Anna shook her head. "You have a lot to learn. Lewis, sometimes I wonder how you could have gotten where you are." She grinned and took out the makeup tray. "I definitely think we have to practice."

"Just make sure both cats and the dog stay inside on the night of the party," Carey instructed Mollie. "We don't want to give Cindy any more excuses."

Cindy made a face.

On the night of the dance there was a full moon and a warm breeze. Borrowing her sister's shawl and wearing an old-fashioned bonnet that her mother had made for her, along with a ruffled blouse and skirt, Cindy looked nothing like the tomboy she was.

"You look great!" Grant said when he picked her up. He was wearing an old top hat and tails that had belonged to his grandfather.

"So do you," Cindy acknowledged.

He took her hand. She hadn't expected to feel so happy and carefree. What was there to worry about?

At school the gym had been made over to look

like the Tennessee hills, and Cindy was amazed at
the transformation. She was also amazed at how
many people were there.

"You think this is nice? You should have seen
the decorations at the Alta California Ball. Whoever's in charge of design tonight did a great job."

Cindy flushed. "I think that's Steve. He's the
one Mollie's been interested in," she blurted out
without thinking.

"That's strange. I know for a fact he's been
dating Barbara Cameron all year."

"Oh." She took the glass of fruit punch he handed
her. "I guess Mollie didn't know that."

"Don't worry. There're plenty of freshmen and
sophomore guys who'll be attracted to your little
sister."

"Yeah"—Cindy smiled—"I don't doubt that."

"Come on." He pulled her onto the dance floor.
"They're doing a Virginia reel."

"But I—"

"You'll pick it up easily. I promise."

Grant was right. She did learn it easily, and
enjoyed the dance, as well as the rest of the
evening.

It really wasn't much different from a party,
Cindy thought as Grant drove her home.

They stopped at the beach and, like two kids,
waded in the surf, ran up and down the sandy
shore, and generally had a good time.

After a while they sat down on the rocks and

Grant's arm went around her. Cindy waited, but to her surprise he didn't immediately try to kiss her. Grant was her boyfriend and her friend, Cindy realized happily. And so they sat, just watching the full moon and listening to the sounds.

While Cindy and Nicole slept late the following morning, Mollie was up early. After all, she thought, pitying herself, she hadn't been to the dance. In fact, she'd probably never get to a dance at Vista. Not at the rate she was going.

Imagine, Steve was dating someone else all along and he hadn't even let on.

She picked up her new issue of *Young Miss*. The quiz this month was how to tell if a boy was the right one for you.

From the desk by the phone, Mollie found a pen that wrote, and curled up on the couch with the afghan her grandmother had made. Methodically, she checked off each question and then, using her dad's calculator, read off the scores.

Well, no wonder Steve hadn't responded to her charms, she thought. He hadn't been right for her at all.

Mollie began to chew at the tip of the pen. She wondered about that guy Nicole had mentioned—Raymond. Now that Nicole was back to being Nicole, she'd ask her sister to bring her to a yearbook meeting. There was always the Winter Ball. And maybe . . .

Here's a glimpse of what you'll find in ALWAYS A PAIR, book five in the "Sisters" series for GIRLS ONLY.

Cindy rolled over and looked at the clock. It was nearly eleven o'clock. She couldn't believe it. Her parents had let her sleep in. She stretched lazily and lay on her bed thinking about the incredible whale-watching trip she'd gone on with her biology class the previous day. It had been thrilling watching those magnificent whales moving through the water. There was something exciting and dangerous about being so close to something so big and powerful.

She wished Grant hadn't been so stubborn and had gone with her. Oh, well, she thought, he would be sorry when she told him what he'd missed.

The phone was ringing and she heard Mollie say, "I don't think she's up yet."

She quickly rolled out of bed. "Yes I am. Is it for me?" Cindy called.

"Here she is." Mollie frowned and handed her the phone.

"Hello." Cindy carried the phone into her room.

"Cindy, it's me, Anna. How were the whales?"

"Awesome." Cindy fell back onto her bed.

"Awesome enough to miss the big dance?"

"You bet. It was the thrill of a lifetime."

"Well, you let Grant give the thrill of a lifetime to Karie Simons last night."

Cindy felt her throat close up. "What are you talking about?" Her hand shook.

"He took Karie to the dance. Didn't he tell you he was taking someone else?"

"No, I guess it never came up." Cindy tried acting nonchalant. "I mean, I told him to ask someone else if he really wanted to."

"I'm sorry, Cindy. I thought you already knew, or I'd have kept my mouth shut."

"It doesn't matter, really. I don't own Grant, you know." Cindy laughed nervously. "And he doesn't own me. We both do whatever we want."

"You're taking this pretty well. I'd be furious."

"I would be, too, if it mattered that much. But it's no big deal," she said a lot more casually than she felt. She then asked several questions about the dance, although she couldn't have cared less. She wasn't about to let Anna know that, though, or how hurt she was that Grant could replace her so quickly. And with Karie Simons, of all people! She was so scatter-brained.

Setting the phone back in the hallway, Cindy practically collided with Nicole coming out of the bathroom. "Who was that?" Nicole asked, toweling off her hair.

"Anna."

"Oh. I saw her at the dance last night," Nicole said carefully. She wasn't sure whether to forge ahead and tell Cindy about Grant or to wait and see if Grant might call and tell her himself.

"She tells me that I was about the only one who missed the dance last night."

"Oh, you heard?"

"You saw him too, then?"

"Yes. I said hi, but he spent most of the night trying to avoid me, I think."

"Well, I hope she was worth it," Cindy snapped.

"And he probably hopes your whales were worth it," Nicole retorted.